W9-CXM-315

How Aliens Think

Johns Hopkins: Poetry and Fiction | *John T. Irwin, General Editor*

How Aliens Think

~~~~~~~~~~~~~~~~~~~

Stories by Judith Grossman

The Johns Hopkins University Press | Baltimore and London

This book has been brought to publication with the generous
assistance of the G. Harry Pouder Fund.

The Johns Hopkins University Press
2715 North Charles Street
Baltimore, Maryland 21218-4363
www.press.jhu.edu

Library of Congress Cataloging-in-Publication Data

Grossman, Judith, 1937–
    How aliens think / Stories by Judith Grossman.
    p.   cm.
    ISBN 0-8018-6171-3 (alk. paper)
    I. Title.
PS3557.R6724H69   1999
813'.54—DC21   99-10689 CIP

A catalog record for this book is available from the British
Library.

Contents

PREFACE

LOOKED AT ONE WAY, these stories follow—sometimes at a distance, sometimes more closely—the writer's own travels, beginning in England, with excursions to other places and times in the Old World, and moving on to an immigrant's life in America. Looked at another way, they trace a long and happy preoccupation with what we can know, or imagine, of the people among whom we live: what is called, in philosophy, "the problem of other minds."

Two narratives, "Great Teacher" and "Death of the Mother," derive more from memory than invention (yet we know that memory creates its own inventions). And one, "De Maupassant's Lunch: An Education," has an acknowledged historical source. For the rest, I offer thanks to the noble art of fiction and the world at large.

How Aliens Think

The Two of You

~~~

YOU HAVE THIS CHARACTER on your hands, and her name is Clara Diamant. Starting right there, she's a character you've been generous to, insofar as the operating rules permit you to be generous. Perhaps it's because you imagine you'd really like to have been born a Ms. Diamant, in another place, time, or gene pool. It's O.K. to be envious of a fiction, isn't it? Certainly, you think, better than being envious of your own child.

Brilliantly endowed is Clara, a rising academic star in her early thirties, just now granted early tenure at Adams University, and scheduled to spend next year as a visiting scholar at Princeton. Her current studies are in Passion and Desire, oh—and the Body, that site of perennial contest between objective and subjective understandings. Clara has also (and why not?—for these things are not forbidden under the rules.) the dark, quicksilver beauty of a new-generation Paulette Goddard. She wears a standard eighties warm-up suit, but her hair's washed and shining with a touch of gel, her nails shaped to an oval and buffed.

This morning, Clara sits in her modest saltbox-style house outside of Boston. Winter sunshine causes small avalanches of snow to slip off the pine branches, which toss up a flurry of wet, green needles and a bright spray of crystals. Clara catches the movement outside her window, looks up for a second absently, then goes back to work on the draft of her chapter concerning what's commonly called "perversion." Beside her is Roland Barthes's celebration of the alternatives to standard heterosexual and procreative practice, on the grounds that they render one simply *more happy*.

Barthes has made a potent observation, she thinks. No one can fail to be moved by the prospect of ways to become *more happy*. On the other hand, here's this opposing view from Luce Irigaray: *Perversion, says Irigaray, which is often touted as a means of escape from repressive morality, remains the slave to a morality of sexual difference that's traditionally organized in a hierarchy....*

Well yes, it's true that what worked for the gay Roland Barthes may not work for the heterosexual woman. Clara's own experience comes back to her suddenly, of living under the rule of an ancient male fear of women's genital strangeness. Growing up in a rabbinical household, she learned about concealment of all things to do with menstruation, and the shame of admitting each month precisely when she became untouchable. She understands, too, what Irigaray's talking about here—the delegation to women of certain "tasks" of sexual fulfilment. The more she reflects, the more considerations arise for her to figure in, and she searches intently along her bookshelves, pulling down Lacan on female sexuality, plus her sunflower-colored copy of *Differences: The Phallus Issue* (a collector's item, that one). There'll be a bow also to Freud, who has contrived to stay scandalous for almost a century now, first for his insights, later for his magnificent inventiveness.

As for her data from the American cultural side, she has a wild mix laid out on the desk. A piece from *Playboy*, detailing the essentials of a good blow job, and how that operation keeps Hollywood running. Mailer's *The Deer Park*, Roth's *Portnoy*, well decorated with Post-its; and Updike's *Couples*, with its celebration of cunnilingus in terms of Christian self-abnegation, a mystical rising up, through descent. These guys are no problem, however: a head like hers, well versed in Talmudic interpretation, should have no trouble sorting them out.

But hurry! you're telling yourself now, as you explore Clara's academic idyll. Because time's going by, and whenever your imagination slows down for a moment, the pack of mental wolves that's been so long on your trail starts closing in, as it always does. And now because there's this dream, this nightmare, that's been forcing its way into your waking life . . .

YOU ARE SITTING IN A VAN, which, it seems, is taking patients just released from a remote mental hospital back to civilization. The driver has missed his way and followed an unpaved road that dead ends here, between a great oak tree and somebody's homestead, between pastures and a garden of vegetables and flowers. The van stops for the driver to get directions. As you get out with the rest, still wearing your striped lunatic's pajamas, you notice a tall blond man with an ax in his hand, walking from the garden.

The task of this blond man is, simply put, to kill you. It makes perfect sense of course, because he looks just like Rutger Hauer in *Blade Runner*. But all the same, it seems unfair just when you're getting your life back, your freedom!

So, you dash for the oak tree, and in a burst of adrenaline you haul yourself up into the high branches that'll never bear his weight. He stands on a lower branch, laughing at you, because where else can you go now? At that you start swinging yourself, like an inspired gibbon, hand-by-hand down the far side of the tree, and jump to the ground at a safe distance. Now *you're* laughing, because you know you can get away.

Only it's not over. The guy with the ax is standing there beside the tree. He rests the ax head on the ground, looks at you, and beckons.

No no, you think, *forget it!* But he walks very deliberately over to a raised bed of flowering pansies, looks at you again, and lays himself face down upon it, as if to demonstrate something. Then you observe another bed of pansies, next to the first. It appears to be just your size. Covered with velvety purple flowers, it invites you, no doubt. You walk slowly over to it and, suddenly tired, lie face down in it, feeling everywhere on your skin the cool petals, breathing the smell of plants, and of earth.

The dream goes dark.

It's true, it stands to reason, that your own father was a man of strikingly blond, Nordic looks. He was raised as a boy by his widowed mother, in poverty, and you remember well the moments when his rage against women's authority peeped through the bars. Sad father, who wrote on your tenth birthday card: *Be good, sweet maid, and let who will be clever.* (But you already knew you couldn't be good, so what was the alternative?) Father who informed you, in your teens, that he would never read any book written by a woman. Father who attempted to remove you from college, on the grounds that you had become sexually immoral. And who died, too soon after that last debacle, for you to try and pacify his resentful ashes, scattered anonymously among the dour evergreens of the Bexley Garden of Remembrance.

Coincidentally, our lovely Clara's father, the distinguished Rabbi, prohibited his favorite daughter from taking up graduate studies in religion. She has repaid him for this offense by marrying a non-Jew, and at present her parents and she barely communicate with each other. So, you and Clara might have something to discuss, between the two of you. Why, for instance, given those bitter quarrels with the father, are both of you committed heterosexuals—indeed, married with children? (Clara has two sons, by the way.)

One answer: in these matters, the body's response is the independent, undeniable, and final judge. Presented with a possible suitor here, another there, it says *No* to this one, and *Yes* to that, and there is no appeal once the trial's been made. A second answer might be the curiosity that drives Clara in her profession, and you in yours. That tropism towards the unknown, the *stranger*, has always been irresistible to both of you. Clara, no doubt, would recognize here what Irigaray calls "the passion of wonder," in the encounter with the Other whose sexual difference will always renew his strangeness.

You would add, for yourself, a third answer: It's essential for the chosen one to show the marks of some bitter suffering, through which the image of your first-loved mother is also affirmed—and they must be *real* scars, on which you find yourself compelled to lay consoling and desiring hands. (Here, you remember a perpetually unhealed sore on one man's leg, carried for all the years you knew him in token of a guilty memory: his failure to get a drink of gin on a Sunday night for his father, in pain from terminal liver cancer—the glass of gin that was the only thing the dying man thought could help him; and the boy went asking in the neighborhood, but to no use, and in the wet evening he fell down some unlighted steps, scraped his leg, and gave up; and his father was gone before morning. You remember too, from another time, a desolate look that called your name.)

But you don't intend to lay these troubles on your Clara. She's the lucky one, and she will, she *must*, enjoy all the freedoms of the generation that succeeded your own. Except that you know the rules demand . . . a little something, just a minor problem here.

You notice that Clara sometimes rubs the right side of her jaw as she works. She's had TMJ syndrome ever since a minor car accident that you gave her in her teens (well, those things are so common . . .), and that left her with a chronic tension around the jaw. Not improved, of course, by her own tendency towards perfectionism. The net result is a certain erotic disability, awkwardly relevant to this chapter she has in hand: to be brutal about it, Clara's just no good at fellatio. She can scarcely get her picture-perfect set of teeth far enough apart for the purpose, or sustain that minimum degree of stretch for longer than a minute or two at a time (which is guaranteed to mess up a partner's rhythm, let alone the way that a sensitive organ takes fright at the mere scrape of a canine). And, frankly, no amount of practice with a banana or a Coke bottle is likely to change the situation.

Clara's luck has reasserted itself in the fact that Terry, her husband, is British and can live quite contentedly on a modest ration of oral stimulation. It's a pleasant feature of Europeans that they don't entertain unlimited expectations; you rarely find them crying for the moon. More of a concern is Clara's own hesitation: Can she overcome the consciousness of her own deficiency and reassert mastery through this alternative head-work of analysis and theoretical discourse? Such are the concealed hazards of intellectual production.

Early afternoon in New England, and a thaw has set in motion innumerable trickling threads of snowmelt, converging towards a musical fall into the roadside storm drain, or spreading quietly into shallow pools among the screen of pines and hemlocks between these houses: a springtime wetland. The children will be home from school soon, and Clara is making a list of headings on her pad, to take up tomorrow.

1. Orality and Narcissism. Has anyone correlated the circumstance of bottle-fed cultures vs. nursing cultures with later sexual practices? Easier to see transition from bottle- to penis-sucking (and cf. Irigaray's point on sex-and-technology links).

2. N.B. patterns of American puritanism and permissiveness, within which certain practices "count less." Also, the assumption of a male sexual drive *requiring* outlet vs. the residual valuing of female virginity. The woman trades away her own satisfaction for greater control over her partner, & fate. Example: Marlene Dietrich et al.

3. Political implications—*yes*. Where reciprocal sexual practices speak of complementarity, equalizing of difference—the ethos of the '60s and after—our '80s reversion to conservative hierarchies should predict a return of dominance and submission: the one person down on her knees, silenced by her laboring on the singular pleasure of the other . . .

HERE THE CHILDREN ARE at the door, and Clara has eaten nothing since eight this morning, living on coffee and the liquid protein mix that helps keep her a perfect size 6. It's quitting time. She stretches up and outward in her chair, with the wind and no wolves at her back, sure of her ability to do the work, and the rightness of it. And when Clara stands, the room becomes magnetized around her.

For you, of course, it feels otherwise: one's self appears always among a plurality of beings, as a tree stands in a grove with other trees. Nor have you ever felt yourself to be more than a technically separate organism. Consciousness is perpetually under compromise, as in the way your voice, speaking on the telephone, involuntarily assimilates to the voice on the other end, or in the way your expression adapts silently to that of your companion.

As R. said, in 1964, *I can look into your face in the morning, and tell exactly how I am feeling that day*.

On the other hand, you don't fear the existence of the Other in the world—the sense that having the mere status of one among Others, instead of occupying the throne of unchallenged Subject, could produce a loss of all meaning in your life. Your terrors are more practical, concerning what the unlimited acquisitive drive of corporate power can do to drive you and yours under. And that someone out there, to whom you represent a hated version of the Other, may care enough to destroy you . . .

OH, NOW YOU *do* wish that you were Clara, safe in her pristine, fictive world, splendidly equipped the way Thetis prepared her Achilles, armed and equal to anything. Only the rules don't work that way; and as Thetis might have known, they never did. Clouds are gathering over the future of Clara's story: next summer, while she goes off traveling, giving papers and receiving applause, her husband will begin an affair with their neighbor, the charming ex-dancer. When it comes out, things could go very wrong, very quickly, given Clara's rapid-fire temperament. She'll be off to Princeton; and with her husband's record of caring for the boys while she travels, who'd give much for her chances of custody? And so on . . .

But there's still time for you to make a pause, to decide that Clara will stay right on course. Her book will be widely acclaimed, professional success continues, her marriage comes through, and prospers. The only cost is that she'll remain a minor character, forever.

A career path is not a story.

All you can offer her is a parting gift, in consolation. It will arrive twelve years into her future, when she's canceled a summer conference date to attend her younger son's concert at music camp, deep in the Berkshire hills. The program runs from Haydn and Mozart to Mendelssohn and Brahms, including duets, trios, quartets, and more, for strings and piano. She sits in the audience, in an old barn with its doors open to the mild air, wearing a pink suit, stockings, and pumps —an outfit she now realizes is too hot and formal for the occasion. Dusk is already gathering when the first chamber group comes on; it will be nearly midnight when the last is rapturously applauded.

The performers are a mix of girls, their dark or blond hair tied back or floating loose, their uniformly long white skirts evoking portraits of Victorian maidens, and boys, blond, russet, or dark, whose all-white shirts and trousers turn them into luminous swains, grouped under the dim hayloft. It's a kind of musical bridal feast. But if Clara looks down, she'll see that many of the players have bare feet, a little mudstained from the afternoon shower, and all the more adorable; and others wear, as adorably, white crew socks with stained white sneakers. They'll play as if their hearts and lives are to be given away entirely, this night. Some girls have the features of young warriors, swinging their violins up to their necks as one might raise a crossbow to shoot; some boys have the slimness of birches and a delicacy of gesture that makes everyone hush and lean forward.

Clara's life has been so focused in another context, she doesn't know anybody here except her Mark, the violist son in question—not even his friends (and her husband went to the conference in her place). At the reception earlier, she talked a little with Mark, who told her it'd been a great time, but he was thinking he'd switch to playing guitar once he finished high school. Clara expressed sorrow and complete surprise. Why would he want to throw away such talent, ten years of learning—and all this besides? Mark only rolled his eyes and went into the old routine of anti-violist jokes:

How can you tell when the stage is level? When the violist is drooling out of both sides of his mouth.

How do you know when a violist is playing out of tune? When the bow's moving.

A conductor and a violist are standing in the middle of the road. Which one do you run over first? The conductor. Business comes before pleasure.

Give her credit, Clara not only loves Mark dearly but can acknowledge where her command of the world, of information, ends. Mark showed her the boundary right there; and minutes later she was still painfully figuring: *business before pleasure?* He was pulled away then, by one of these proud girls sweeping their white skirts carelessly through the grass, even before she could tell him—break a leg.

Clara takes her place here in the audience, yet as usual, set apart from the ambient conversation by her own poise, containment—the whole carapace of her disciplined, professional self. But what she feels most keenly is how *hard* it is for her, suddenly, to feel this—the wild intimacy of those lovely adolescents: the intense aura of so much unguarded feeling, such hotly whispered sexuality. She is used to students, after all. But out here, in the hills—what it is, is something else.

Early in the concert, a quartet sweeps in, takes up position, and holds its gaze intently on the red-headed first violin for the slight nod of a cue. Then, in unison, they break into this baroque palace of a piece, like playful barbarians. Now they glance up from the music to make rapid eye contact, verifying their place in the dance; and again, one of the players flips a page quickly, at a pause. Equally partners and challengers of each other, they continue raising the drama of every tonal shift, until with the final movement, the red-headed violinist's arrogance pushes reckless speed to the edge of chaos. But they make it, they reach the final chord, hold it to the very end, and rise for the ceremonial bow—once, twice—before falling apart into disbelieving laughter.

Clara applauds as long as possible, for that's her son, the violist, and so far as she can tell, he's done all right. Then they're gone, and in their place are an impossibly handsome Russian boy at the piano with a very young Korean girl violinist. No smiles, this time, nothing but the sombre dedication of late Brahms. But Clara has already surrendered, in the darkness of the dark-timbered barn, filled with such an endless harvesting of sound and feeling. Clara, who at forty-two hasn't cried since before graduate school, who takes immense pride in the fact that she's kept composure in the face of the world at all times, lays down her arms and takes your gift of tears gratefully, in silence.

From the Old World:
Four Lives from a Saga

~~~

Consistency, continuity, and sameness of experience provide
a rudimentary sense of ego identity.
ERIK ERIKSON, *Childhood and Society*

BEFORE THE PRESENT AGE of depopulated families, you would typically have, as in our case, your straight uncle and your bent one. These two were born seven years apart, far from the heartland, in a region suffering from a deep depression. Soon after the birth of the bent uncle, their father died. Naturally, given the well-established connection between fatherlessness and bentness. The death itself was also natural—that's to say, it came about from causes familiar in those parts, namely bronchial pneumonia complicated by understandable discouragement. Basically, over work conditions: the dark, the fumes, the falling rocks. And then the lack of work, lack of cash, the shoes worn out, the wet weather, and everlasting cold, cold, cold.

There were other brothers in the family; never mind them as yet.

Straight Uncle Frank went to the city young and worked double shifts in Phillips' Brewery, sending money home every week. His growth became stunted as a natural result of hard labor and short rations: he lived mainly on chip butties, eaten from newspapers leaking ink, plus the free beer. He fell in love with a girl from the tenements, Dottie. Despite his short legs and greyish complexion, she recognized his sterling qualities and would become engaged to him for the next eleven years.

Meanwhile Uncle Raymond, who proved to be the clever one of the family (*vide* the often noted connection between bentness and cleverness), began to learn Latin under the tutelage of a local clergyman who took a particular interest. One night, his Mam looked over his shoulder and said, after a minute, "What's that you're reading?"

"It's Ovid, Mam. Latin poetry."

The next night, going to read further, he found that section of the book torn out.

"Mam!' he called, in distress. "There's pages torn out of my Latin book."

And she said, "I know. I did it."

"But why, Mam?"

"Because it's filth, and I'll not have it in the house."

And he said, "I never knew you could read Latin, Mam."

"I know enough," she said (having her wits about her all right), "to know what's filth."

The clergyman arranged to send Raymond to the city for his schooling. He declared: "I'll not stand by and see a good mind wasted."

It had been his fondest hope to see the boy go to college. But the people Raymond was sent to board with were spiteful and mocked everything from his Northern accent to his attempts to steal small items from them—the odd handkerchief or shelf ornament. He developed a nervous asthma; his throat clammed up and he couldn't tell his lies above a whisper. So he went to live with straight Uncle Frank, and lacking the power of voice, he began a course in commercial art. For that boy had all the talents. Sadly, though, as his voice returned, he lost interest in art. And the clergyman by now had lost interest in Ray, who, being too clever for any job that might be offered him, soon wandered in paths other than those that were straight.

As the brother who went into the Postal Service put it, Raymond was more or less on the fringes of respectable society—i.e., bent. By this time, of course, Frank's savings had enabled his mother and the rest to move south, to the city and its opportunities.

MEANWHILE THE EXPECTED AUNTS—the kind and the cruel, according to custom—were born into the other side of the family, residing in the featureless district south of the brewery. At the christening of Edith, the precious first-born of her parents' union, all admired the child's angelic beauty. It's been thought she may have undertaken the role of "cruel aunt" voluntarily, in a spirit of sacrifice. Somebody had to do it, and rather her dear self than somebody worse. (Then again, *nota bene* the traditional linkage between beauty and cruelty . . .)

As she grew up, everyone recognized her striking resemblance to that idol of the day, Princess Frederika Louise. In keeping with her innate distinction, she could never stomach the family's coarse food—their bread and dripping, their suet puddings. The doctor prescribed, for her chronic gastritis, a diet of steamed sole, poached chicken, junkets. Which the parents did their best to supply, though such luxuries meant an end to family outings on Bank Holidays, and the younger children had to wear shoes that were either too big (for growing into) or too small (you'll get some for Easter). But never mind them.

Kind Aunt Madge, born two years after Edith, and with weak eyes and Brillo-pad hair, was destined for the role of her sister's bondservant—naturally, given a common belief of the time, that it's only one per cent of people that are born to rule; the rest are born to obey.

Madge's schooling came to an early end, after she was placed next to Thelma who told jokes in class, out of the side of her mouth, and dirty rhymes like *Lottie Collins has no drawers, would you kindly lend her yours?* that had her in stitches. At the third offense of being caught laughing (later, she had to wonder what it was about Thelma —only a common girl, as Edith pointed out), she was ordered up to the office. The Head sent a letter home by way of sister Edith, for security reasons. As they walked together, Madge begged and begged Edith just to drop the letter quietly down a drain. Nobody would find out; everyone knew they never bothered.

But Edith went straight on. She had, after all, an unprecedented perfect record in school for both achievement and conduct, which she could hardly be expected to let down.

Their mother read it first and said: "Your father'll have something to say about this." And when he came in from work and had washed up, he read it and told Madge: "Get upstairs and take off that dress."

Then he drank his tea, took off his belt, and went up after her, and my goodness she caught it on the bare behind. In later life, Madge would occasionally tell about this and say: "I can't ever for—"

And there'd come a pause, as if expecting the word *forgive*, but instead she would continue: "No, I can't ever forget that."

Once Madge turned fifteen, she left school to get work as a clerk-typist, like so many. And it was not a moment too soon, because Edith was to go on to teachers' college, and every bit of Madge's salary was needed to help with costs.

Now the various siblings of these families emerged on the urban hinterlands to live as they could, and the story of them and their offspring, who became in due course civil servants, sales assistants, home help aides, and draftsmen, will have to be told elsewhere, or not.

But the brother who came after Frank and the sister who came after Madge met and married, and through moderate procreation gave title to the set of aunts and uncles that included the cruel, the straight, the bent, and the kind.

After the death (natural, but not easy) of his mother, Frank married his sweetheart, Dottie. They left for a four-day honeymoon in Ireland, wearing the new drip-dry clothing you can rinse out in hotel sinks. We have photos of Dottie in her aqua Courtelle two-piece, her salmon-and-white check Courtelle dress, etc., and one of Frank featured as human interest in a view of Dublin Bay, from Howth.

No children were born to them. Instead, it was Raymond who occupied their second bedroom between expeditions. *Our home will always be your home* were the words spoken. Meanwhile, Ray was settling into his dual career as freelance accountant and clergyman. To give him his due, he was never accused of shaming the cloth. Nor was his advice on financial matters by any means despised: several persons did extremely well out of it—although when the time came, they preferred not to bear witness at his trial.

In due course Ray was wrongfully acquitted of the charges brought. Still, one newspaper at least hailed him as "a noted confidence-man." He went for a while to Brazil, where he bought his macaw, Creaky, one of the last speakers of the language of an extinguished Indian tribe. At first, to recoup his investment, he rented the magnificent bird out to some linguistic anthropologists, but over time, and without ever having read M. Flaubert, he became more attached to Creaky than to any other sentient being. In beauty, none (not even Aunt Edith) could compete: his breast plumage was a radiant yellow-gold, his back a soft paradisal green, shading over his wings and tail to sapphire blue. And whether perched erect on his stand or hanging one-footed upside down working on a pistachio nut, he had a dignity, that bird. A demeanor.

That was a good decade for the family. Aunt Edith attained the height of her career, with her appointment as head of a special school for slow and handicapped learners. Her systematic approach to erasing educational problems produced remarkable results. It was only weak-minded administrators that prevented its wider adoption. Even so, Edith seemed on the brink of national recognition when one evening, tragically, her car was rammed by a driver with whom she'd had an altercation at a traffic light. Permanently disabled, she retired on her pension close to Aunt Madge, whose husband died about that time and whose only child had emigrated to South Africa.

"My life is ruined," Edith said, "but at least you are left to me."

(The remaining sisters had already taken advantage of Aunt Edith's several offers never to speak to them again, followed by a slam-down of the phone.)

Next to die, as Christmas followed Christmas too soon for the bottles of Drakkar Noir to be used up (or in some cases even opened) was Uncle Frank. His wife had so loved him that she kept on making his favorite charred steaks and pickled beets even after his stomach went bad. He refused chemotherapy, on the grounds that it would make too much trouble for everyone, and passed away one year before retirement.

He was much missed. The soul of goodness always—no, he was, he really was. Never a cross word.

It's nobody's fault, is it, that there's so little to say about such a completely decent person?

And now Dottie sold up and moved to Frinton, where her mother had a bungalow, leaving Raymond and his bird homeless. Well, what did he expect? For a while he lived in his van, then in a lock-up garage he rented for storing things—small appliances, whatever came his way. In one corner he had a screen round a spare car-seat for a bed, the birdcage over the foot of it, and an electric fire for heating. So far, so good, he thought, under the circumstances. But it was a hard winter that year, and while he was out making some deal or other that took more time than anticipated, the fuse on the fire blew, and Creaky, his learned and beautiful macaw, died in the freezing darkness.

Thus bereft, Ray continued on. And was taken in by a lady from the West Indies, whom the family never really got to know, though they certainly appreciated what she did for Ray. One day he was sitting on the couch in her flat, wheezing a little from the emphysema that was gaining on him and thinking that despite this broiling summer that prize bitch Dottie was never going to invite him down to the bungalow, when it seemed as if a voice out of the overheated air summoned him to write his life story—the unique tale of his ups and downs in the world.

One of the nephews who paid Raymond a visit once or twice a year noticed a pile of notebooks growing in the flat. Also they'd go for a lager and lime in the pub 'round the corner, and Ray's friends would be joshing him about what he was putting in that there book of his. But then we heard about his sudden heart attack, and after the cremation the West Indian lady who'd taken him in asked the family what they wanted to do about Ray's clothes and things, and the upshot was that it all got put out for the Salvation Army.

A DECADE AND MORE LATER, Aunt Madge and Aunt Edith faced each other across the Yuletide dinner table. Madge had come in the night before to wash and set Edith's naturally wavy hair that remained so silky and never went grey at all, and she cut Edith's toenails that she herself hadn't seen in years and massaged her poor legs tormented by agonies beyond the power of doctors to comprehend or

to relieve (though the too-rarely-offered shot of Demerol was gratefully received). Madge had slept little, wrapped in blankets on the
carpet, and this morning had prepared the meal: roast, stuffed pheas-
ant, steamed potatoes, and brussels sprouts, currant sauce, and a
mince pie to follow.

Edith spoke. "Not easy to ruin a simple roast, is it dear? But I'll
honestly admit, you found a way."

They continued eating. Afterwards, Madge washed up, cleaned
off the stove, rinsed and hung the dishcloth out to dry, and returned
to the sitting room. At once a kind of warm numbness infused the
left side of her head and neck.

"Oh! I'm not feeling well," she said, reaching with her right hand
for the armchair and dropping into it.

"That's indigestion," Edith came back smartly. "Can't say I'm surprised."

"Afraid I can't hear you, dear."

Edith raised her voice. "It's because you're getting old!"

And at some imperceptible moment in the next few hours, the
kind Madge became as old as she would ever be.

She was much loved. Her son even phoned from Johannesburg,
"very distressed" that he wouldn't be at the funeral. His company director couldn't spare him even for two days, business was so good.

There was a small turnout, not many flowers either, but it was a
bad time of year for flowers. The poor vicar obviously didn't quite
know what to say, because to be honest Madge wasn't much of a
churchgoer. Somehow he managed, of course: it's their job, isn't it?

But as for our Aunt Edith, she lived forever after, for as long as a
cruel heart could desire, and even longer.

"Rovera"

~~~

To die for the love of boys. What could be more beautiful?
MICHEL FOUCAULT, reported by D. A. Miller

Vera & baby Ian (2 wks.), arriving "Rovera."
That was her homecoming outfit, a butter-yellow pique two-piece: impractical for a new mother, but it *was* pretty. Vera stood under the rustic pokerwork sign, waiting while Robert backed and edged the car into the tiny driveway and feeling no impatience, just infinite gratitude for being home at last. Only when Robert came along the path, holding his Brownie camera, then her eyes brimmed. She tilted her head a little towards the baby and smiled for the picture. Blessedly, she had her body to herself again now, and this wee treasure too.

"Another quick snap, OK?"

The tears she blinked away weren't so much for the pain, or the awful, well, *immodesty* of giving birth, but two weeks on that maternity ward, with nineteen other mothers and their squalling bundles in cots at the end of each bed, had left her cruelly exhausted, and shocked to the heart. They were treated like—they *were* like—cows lined up in a milking barn. And what some of those women talked about, joked about, was not to be believed.

Never again; once was enough: she and Robby were in full agreement on that.

With Ian, in any case, they had all they needed. People said boys were harder, but this one was just a sweet little moaner compared to those bellowing bull calves in the hospital. She carried the baby upstairs to the back bedroom, which was fitted out with a chest of drawers and changing table (used, but Robby had sanded and painted them a pristine white), cot (new), and a rocking chair by the window where she could feed him. In half an hour she was settled there with her cup of tea on the sill and a clean nappy draped over the breast the baby was working on.

While he was so engaged, or when he was being changed and wiped, he was "the baby." Other times, as when propped up among cushions for a photo, he was their son, Ian, who would grow up to be a person (only without her nose, she hoped—too much of a good thing, there—or Robert's chin—too little of that, bless him).

With her free hand, she put aside the voile curtain to see how the Hockneys' summer house next door was coming along. They'd planned it for Dave, their twelve-year-old with TB, to be out in the fresh air. And what a pathetic affair it was! Six feet across at most, supported by rustic-style poles that a March wind could blow down, trellising halfway up the sides, and a pointy roof clapped on top. Today, the carpenter was wedged inside with his behind sticking out, fitting a couple of benches.

The baby pulled his mouth off her breast with a sudden pop. She looked down and laughed at those big eyes—he'd surprised himself, hadn't he? The door creaked—that was her Robert. He asked if he could come in before he put his head 'round, so humbly bashful about it, as if she and the baby were a kind of royalty. Like a St. Joseph in the Nativity scene—and in a way she liked that, but in another way, somehow not so much.

Robert tackling garden, Sept. '32

Every fine weekend he was out there, getting it under control, cutting back the overgrown hydrangeas and forsythia along the path. Back and forth he went with the secateurs and a rake, making piles at the back of the garden to burn; and Vera took Ian out between naps to watch his father work.

Afternoons, the baby could sleep in his pram outside, unless the wind blew the bonfire smoke towards the house. There was also a problem if the smoke blew towards the Hockneys', because the sick boy was parked out there in the summer house, wrapped in a blanket, even on overcast days. The sound of his coughing penetrated, like some irritating machine set to go off every few minutes: a cough, then another cough, and a rasping effort to clear the phlegm out of his throat. He had a little bowl to spit in, on the round table between the benches. She avoided looking at it, even from a distance over the fence. Mrs. Hockney would regularly hand him in something to drink, but Vera had yet to hear her say more to him than, "Here you are, Dave; don't forget your medicine." The father came out once in a weekend to mow the lawn, or just to look at it and tell Rob he wished the whole thing could be cemented over; then he'd stop by the summer house to tell the boy to "buck up there"—or words to that effect. They had a second child, Alice, named after the Princess Royal, who played only in the front garden or down the road with her friends.

Robby had mentioned before how it bothered him, Dave being left out there by himself all the time, with only a book or a jigsaw puzzle on a tray.

"I can understand it to an extent, their being worried about the infection. But wouldn't you think they could do a bit more for the lad?"

Vera agreed completely; and weekdays it must be worse, since he couldn't go to school. But you couldn't say anything. Even a friendship with these neighbors was out of the question: not only were they distinctly better off (Mr. H., who was with Internal Revenue, played golf on Saturdays), but they'd hung an expensive metal plaque over their porch, with "St. Ives" in Gothic letters, which made an unfortunate contrast with Robert and Vera's notion of melding their own names to make "Rovera." Nobody likes being shown up as, well, naive.

"To me, it's that you never hear him complain."

"No," she said, "you don't, do you?"

Once the garden was organized, Robert suggested to the Hockneys that he could teach Dave how to build a model aeroplane. Along with playing the violin, this had been a favorite hobby of his before his marriage. He'd pay for the supplies—balsa wood, glue, tissue paper, and so on—out of his own pocket, and he already had the tools. Once Dave got the hang of it he could amuse himself, perhaps. Mrs. H. jumped at the idea—no surprise to Vera, be it said.

By the time cold weather set in, Rob and Dave had built together a pair of Sopwith Camel biplanes. They had a test launching on a fine, windless day, with the Hockneys standing in a row outside their kitchen door. Vera held the baby up to watch, on the other side of the low hedge. Mr. H. had his camera at the ready.

Great airplane launch, Nov. '32

That was Dave, all wrapped up in two pullovers, a scarf, and a knitted cap, jittering with excitement on the summerhouse step, asking was it ready, could it go now? A sweet-looking boy, sensitive type. Vera appreciated the way he looked up to her husband. Robby was so goodhearted: you could tell, just watching them, what a wonderful father he'd be when Ian got a little older.

He put the ready-wound launcher into Dave's hands, set the biplane's angle, stepped back, and checked his watch. At his word Dave released the crank, the rubber band spun, and the red-and-white plane soared upwards to rooftop height, banking into a wide, elegant loop over the rows of gardens, orbiting there with a featherweight buoyancy, round and round, until Vera's neck got a cramp looking up.

"One minute, ten seconds so far!" Rob announced. The flight was already a triumph. Vera never saw such rapture as she did then on Dave's face. And still the plane flew on and on, in such perfect circles you could hardly tell it was gradually descending.

At one minute, forty seconds it was spiraling visibly tighter, down to a few feet overhead. Another turn, and it just missed the pear tree at the back of the Hockneys', came 'round again, and dived past Vera to clip her washing line loaded with nappies, tumbling end-over-end into the grass. Robert ran back through the alley to retrieve the plane, accompanied by a spatter of applause. He'd explained to Dave the hazards presented by the terrain—too bad they couldn't use the sports field yet. Even so, when he returned with the wing struts on one side hanging down broken, the poor lad was distraught.

"It's O.K., Dave, we'll fix it. Only take an hour."

He put his arm around Dave and gave him a quick sideways hug, but the wheezing only worsened into spasms of choked sobbing. Vera watched—she couldn't say a word—while Rob pulled out his handkerchief and wiped the boy's eyes, his messy face. It took all that time, she observed, for Mrs. H. to get over there and take the boy indoors. And then—Vera put a hand over her mouth, silently screaming "Where's the carbolic? "—Rob stuffed the handkerchief, loaded with germs, right back in his pocket.

For Christmas that year Vera made her husband a dressing gown: it was a lightweight wool plaid, half-lined in taffeta, with piping around the collar and cuffs. She was concerned there might be a misunderstanding between the two of them, Robert being so quiet. But when they'd agreed that one baby was enough, she never thought it meant they wouldn't make love again. There were ways to prevent babies, even she knew. She'd been back to normal three months now, Ian was started on the bottle, and still Rob kept to his side of the bed. Perhaps, if it went on like this, she should speak to Dr. McKechnie.

How to put it into words, though? So difficult— especially with a Scotsman who didn't waste words himself. Also, she didn't mean to complain, when Robert was so good to them, bringing home his weekly pay envelope and putting it right on the table for allocation according to their budget, with a small allowance for his lunches and cigarettes. He got up every morning without fail to take out the ashes and start the boiler. Put out the bins. Gave her an affectionate kiss on the cheek when he left in the morning *and* another when he came in the door at twenty-five past six. A truly devoted father, too, if awkward at showing it. The way he'd befriended poor Dave, anybody could tell. He even sent an extra Christmas card next door, specially for the boy.

Dec. 25, '32: Robt. & baby Ian, aged 6 mos
On Christmas Day, after they got home from his widowed mother's house (every year Vera brought over the pudding and the mince pie, and every year it was no comment), she had Robert try on the dress-

ing gown. The size was perfect. Did he like it? He said of course, it was beautiful, almost too good to wear for everyday. No, but he must wear it, that was what it was *for*, she said.

Vera picked up the camera, for once, put the baby in Rob's arms, and while Ian in that thoughtful way of his leaned back to study his dad's face, she took the flash picture. When the baby was in bed, she got a small glass of port for each of them, with biscuits, and took the tray into the lounge, where Rob sat leafing through a *National Geographic*. She handed him the glass and stroked across his shoulders, meaning all the time: *See how I love you, Robby? Even besides going to your mother's every Christmas, and not to my own family (which always upsets them), because I know you need me to.*

There was more that she could have said. Wasn't it true that their marriage itself had been his idea—oh, very much so—when she'd been perfectly happy with her secretary's job in the city, being friends and going to concerts together? And now that she'd done it, become his wife, had the baby, and all—well, for the first time she really felt she *deserved* a husband. In bed she made one more try, reaching her arm over him as he lay beside her. He shifted onto his side, facing her, and put his free arm over hers. Their knees, clothed in flannel, bumped together.

"Oh, sorry," he said.

"'S all right."

She moved her hand gently down around his ribs, let it wait tactfully there. A minute or more passed. She heard his breathing slow down, until finally he was asleep and his hand over her elbow relaxed and slid away. Why on earth had she said it was all right, when it wasn't?

Ian meets potty, Apr. '33

Dr. Truby King advised that toilet training should be accomplished by the end of baby's first year. So far, Ian sat on his potty-chair just to please her, without delivering the goods. It seemed an opportunity, when Robert came down with bronchitis, for Ian to be shown the use of the toilet by his Dad, after the worst of the infection was over.

The two of them went off to the bathroom together after breakfast, and sure enough Ian produced a small number two, right in the potty. *That* was a celebration! But only a couple of mornings later, Rob suffered his first hemorrhage. Vera heard him choking, from where she was fastening her stockings in the bedroom. She ran in, and all she could think to do was stuff a clean nappy to his mouth to catch the blood. Then she dashed next door to call the ambulance from Mrs. Hockney's phone, leaving him there on the toilet with poor little Ian beside him.

When she got back, Ian had managed to crawl to the top of the stairs, potty-chair tied to his behind, howling for her. And Rob was still on the bathroom floor, deathly pale, gripping for dear life onto the edge of the bath.

Rob was operated on in the hospital, and Vera's mother came to stay for that time. But there was no use trying to get Ian back on the potty; none of Dr. Truby King's ideas worked. The problem was he'd been put right off it, that was his Gran's opinion, and Vera was afraid she was right. They'd have to wait awhile and try it later, elsewhere in the house perhaps.

They told Vera the bad news: Rob had developed a virulent TB in both lungs: the one that was operated on couldn't be saved, but there might be a chance for the other, caught at this stage.

Easy to see how he got it, of course. If the Hockneys had only put Dave in the sanitarium, where he belonged! And if only Rob hadn't involved himself! But they hadn't, and he had, and no use crying over it. Back home, she went upstairs to Ian's bedroom, where he was napping soundly. Quietly she lifted the corner of the voile curtain and looked down at the summer house, where Dave was lying on two pillows, his head towards her. Mild sunshine lit up the blond hair, drooping uncut over his forehead. *I've got a husband in the hospital, lost one lung already because of you,* she thought, *and I've a child still in nappies. I could just strangle you, you young menace. And your blasted parents, into the bargain.*

Aug. '33: Postcard from Hockneys, Torquay, Devon
The Hockneys moved, at short notice: Internal Revenue habitually switched their officials to different regions every six years or so, to en-

sure honesty. When Rob came home after months of convalescence, he was disappointed to hear they'd left, and he asked how Dave was. Vera said, very shortly, she thought he was much the same.

But it was a shock to see the way Rob looked, creeping between bedroom and bathroom. For him to come downstairs once a day for supper was a heroic journey. Everything he touched had to be cleaned with carbolic, his laundry boiled. Vera's hands and arms up to the elbow became red and cracked, though she used Vaseline constantly to salve them. And the worst was that Ian, now a toddler, wasn't allowed to go closer to Rob than three feet. "Dad" signifed for him this piece of human furniture, parked here or there in the house, kept off limits like the glass cabinet in the lounge, and about as interesting. Ian was an easy child, good as gold. Vera even caught herself using similar language about Rob to the new neighbors: "He's so good, such an easy patient."

She knew, though, watching Rob's eyes, that every breath he drew in frightened him, as if something might tear open inside. Nobody would tell her if he was right. He talked even less than before, mouthing the words so she had to lean over to hear. Reading the morning paper took half his morning; he unfolded it so slowly it maddened her to watch, then repeated the process for every page, painstakingly refolding and unfolding.

Since he'd been put in the little third bedroom, Vera thought about making it more attractive. Some photos on the bureau could make it up to him a little for being kept away from Ian. She went through her box for snapshots of father and son together. There were plenty of pictures of her and Ian, of Ian sitting in his high chair, Ian learning to crawl. But the only decent one she had of father and son together was the snapshot from Christmas, which she'd rather not see again.

She bought a frame set for three pictures: one of the baby sitting up, one of her holding him, and the Christmas photo, and set them on the night table. When they'd been there a few days, Rob asked her if she could put up the snapshot of him launching the plane with Dave. So she took the photo with herself in it out of its frame—as she told Robby, he could see her face any day of the week—and put the other one in. Mr. Hockney's was certainly a much better picture. Well, they could afford a much better camera, to start with.

Jan. '34: Rob't in his chair at the french windows
If he were a dog, the thought flitted through Vera's mind, alone in the kitchen boiling up milk, *we'd have to be thinking about putting him down.*

His mother insisted he had more color in his face, but any sane person could see that for all her efforts Rob was worse off than the day he'd come home. Fevers and sweating every night, and the flesh had melted off him: he wouldn't eat because his throat hurt too much. She made endless milk puddings—rice, custard, and tapioca—but whatever she made, he never finished a bowl. He was going downhill, didn't the doctor see, who came 'round every three weeks to prescribe cough mixture and Friars' Balsam inhalant? And the laundry was a nightmare—blood spots on the handkerchiefs and pillow cases leaving more and more overlapping brown stains, which eventually you couldn't bleach away.

It came to the point that Rob needed help getting out of the bath, even. He hardly ever came downstairs; his meals all had to be taken up. A grown man, to be this feeble? And good Lord, what miserable thoughts must he be thinking? He never said, so she didn't know.

The next time the doctor visited, she asked him to come into the front room for a minute. There she put it to him: Robert was losing ground, and she was at the limit of her strength, running between the patient and the baby.

"Well Mrs. Benskin," he said, "I've only been waiting for you to say the word. I'll put in a request tomorrow, to the sanitarium."

July, '34: Robert taking the sun on terrace, Broadhill
His complexion was nicely tanned, his face had creased itself into a smile, although the body on the lounge chair was just a bony sketch under the striped blanket.

Vera came every Saturday, leaving Ian alternately with her

mother and with Rob's. Since she couldn't drive the car, she took a train and two buses—over two hours each way for a one-hour visit. The bag she carried contained a box of licorice All-Sorts—because each time he'd ask her: "*Have you brought me my Spanish?*"—and the bottle of Sanatogen tonic wine that he liked before supper, and the other bottle, of Chlorodyne, for his stomach. The bottles were individually wrapped in brown paper, then put in a Chisholm's bag to disguise them, for the staff at Broadhill were strict as well as stingy with the medicines they handed out: mostly aspirin and bromides.

"It's no use complaining to them," Robert told her when she protested. "Look at it from their viewpoint: if they started making exceptions to the rules, they'd never stop."

But why shouldn't he have these little comforts, since he wanted them? For the first time, she'd begun to think about how much time he could have left. She took the photo of him then, for Ian's sake as much as for her own, and before she left, remembered the small square envelope that had come for him in the post. He drew his hands slowly out from under the blanket to take it, and edged a fingernail under the flap. Vera made a mental note to bring scissors and file next time, to cut those nails—and the toenails, too. The sheet of paper inside was lined and written on both sides in pencil.

"It's from Dave," he said, clearly pleased.

"Oh, is it?"

Of course she already knew, because of the Devonshire postmark. But why spoil the surprise? Now Robert was reading it, word by word, as she sat and passed her gaze along the row of immobile patients, all propped at a slight angle on their lounges, some apparently asleep, others being talked to by relatives (but the murmuring voices didn't carry in the open air, with the sound of a lawnmower going below the terrace, and farther away a tractor turning hay in a field). Robert turned the sheet over and read to the end.

"He mentions that Sopwith Camel we made, Vera. Says he still has it, keeps it in his room. He's in a sanitarium, too, near the coast. He's making friends, a couple of boys near his own age."

It was a long speech for Robert, and Vera mustered up enthusiasm: how nice of Dave to write, and by the way, did he want her to speak to the doctor about a transfer to somewhere pleasanter than Broadhill?

Robert thought for a minute and finally said not to bother: this was as good a place as any. He'd become friendly with a couple of the other patients—one fellow had been 'round the world twice, working his passage on the P & O liners, had many stories to tell. She said he should think about it anyway, and meanwhile it would be Ian's second birthday on Thursday, so she would bring him next time. Something to look forward to.

Before leaving, Vera checked to see that none of the nurses was around, opened the Chlorodyne bottle, and poured forty drops, counting, into the glass of water beside his lounge. He drank. She tucked the bottle into his carryall, under a book, and waited beside him till he drifted off.

June, '35: Ian on donkey rides, Sandown Bay, Isle of Wight
So many things to be grateful for, despite all. This holiday for one (the first they'd had since Rob became ill), thanks to the life insurance benefit so promptly paid up. Ian's happiness made her life worthwhile: things like feeling the excitement through his hand holding hers, coming up the gangplank onto the ferry boat. As soon as they got back, Vera would have the house sold—the estate agent was showing "Rovera" to prospective families even now—and her secretarial position at St. George's School (C. of E. endowed) would begin in late August. By that time she'd have a flat arranged within walking distance of her mother, who'd take Ian in the daytime till he was old enough for school.

Under the sun and the sea breeze, just cool enough to be comfortable, she felt an enjoyment that had been missing for so long, practically since she was a single girl. Ian, in his white floppy sun hat and swimsuit, was at work in the brown sand with his bucket and spade. Having a deck chair, too, that was well worth the sixpence a day. Vera shaded her eyes and looked down to the shoreline where a small wave folded over, made a small "plash!", thinning out into sand, followed by another, and another, out over a hazy sea to the horizon, and the plume of grey smoke from a steamer, and what was that big boat now, coming into view 'round the headland to the right? Even without binoculars you could see it must be one of the great liners, painted white, with many rows of portholes along the side.

Vera pointed it out to Ian and told him that liner was probably going to India—or Africa—magic names, her voice implied. She drew a big circle in the sand: here's where *they* were, three-quarters up on the left, and here was Europe to the right of them, Africa straight down, and India all the way over there, and he could go to India some day because it belonged to England, and so did a lot of other places.

Ian wanted to know the liner's name, but she couldn't see from such a distance, only guess that it might be a P & O boat. Which brought to mind the friend Robert had mentioned during his last months in the sanitarium who had sailed 'round the world, also the books he'd been reading: memoirs of travel in distant places. When Robert passed away in March without warning (the telegram arrived at eight-thirty A.M.), she went to Broadhill and packed up the few things from his nightstand. On top was *The Seven Pillars of Wisdom*, which he had asked for at Christmas. All the pages were cut, that was his methodical way; and tucked in about two-thirds through as a bookmark was the square envelope with the letter in it from Dave— no, there were two or three letters, so Robert must have had more correspondence with the boy.

Her first thought at the time was to keep the book for Ian to have, later; her second, decisive thought was to donate it to the sanitarium library. It would have had to be fumigated, in any case. The letters she dropped quietly into a waste basket under the nightstand, as none of her business.

For a while after Robert passed away, she would catch herself in a wicked hope that Dave had died of the disease, too. She even considered writing to the Hockneys to find out if he had. Fortunately she'd refrained, so that now, on this wide beach with Ian, she felt no shadow on this little life the two of them were making. When she imagined her mother, or another relative or friend asking her if she would think of getting married again, she absolutely knew her answer: Never. And if they pressed her, asking her why, she had the answer to that too: "I've already got everything I need."

De Maupassant's Lunch: An Education

~~~

But in the center of the largest panel there was a strange thing which caught my eye, a black object in relief against a square of red velvet. I approached it: it was a hand—a man's hand."
GUY DE MAUPASSANT, "The Hand," translated by Lafcadio Hearn

In the 1870s, Maupassant in Paris told versions of this story after dinner: the Goncourt brothers heard it more than once; even Henry James heard it and commented in a letter that the details were "irreproducible." It seems to have involved an encounter, during Maupassant's adolescence, with the English poet Swinburne—also with a monkey, and finally (but who can be sure?) the acquisition of that severed hand which, years later, was still among the writer's possessions, observed lying in his bathroom.

A full century afterwards I happened to be reading Swinburne's letters, for no better reason than that, as a graduate student, I'd quarrelled with Philip Rahv over the merits of these lines:

> Before the beginning of years,
> There came to the making of man
> Time, with a gift of tears,
> Grief, with a glass that ran.

Rahv dismissed the verse as sweetly trivial—I found a bitter aftertaste—and so, by a roundabout process, this story, which neither of us knew at the time, eventually came into my hands . . .

HERE WAS SWINBURNE, the poet, steadying his ink pot on the rustic table in the arbor and choosing a pen from his writing case. Words came to him as always, alas, fluently. "Dearest Mimmie," he wrote. "The late September here is glorious, the beaches scoured clean of summer. This morning it's perfectly calm; however, three days since we had an equinoctial gale that sent me a marvellous sea-adventure."

He paused, to retake the pleasure once more for himself, before giving it away. How an army of waves rushed imperially upon the beach—how they towered, then struck forward—how George wouldn't let him go in swimming that day, and only under protest the next, in the afternoon when they were both drunk, and with the tide receding. As soon as he'd got past the roiling torments of the shingle, he found himself lifted away buoyantly from one wide surge to the next, each crested with a bubbling ripple, a whispered echo of the storm.

When he touched the ebb current, twenty yards out, he knew instantly that there was no chance of fighting it. Even as he called for help, swinging on a course wide of the rocky arch at the point, his cry seemed to him a pure formality.

"I shall die," he thought, "at the same age as Shelley, and in the same manner. An annoying coincidence!"

But so be it: one solicited the Powers, but it was in their own manner that they responded. Thus he went floating naked into the Channel, like a pale-and-russet weed on the swells, looking up at small figures waving hysterically from the clifftop, and beyond them at the fair-weather clouds scudding eastward into Normandy. And only minutes later, the fishing smack came into view, riding a crest; he waved, and heard shouts, and watched it come about, drifting in irons towards him as he swam to meet it.

Two jerseyed fishermen hauled him over the gunwale. "The good God has saved your life for you," one remarked. But he said he'd much prefer to give *them* the credit, and they showed their rotten teeth in pleasure—as again at the discovery that he was an English gentleman, almost a Milord. He was wrapped in an old rusty sail, for decency and for protection against the brisk wind. And on the run back to Yport, he seized the chance of reciting to them radical verses by the great Victor Hugo, to which they listened in astonishment, so that he felt truly as if he'd restored a measure of their poetic birthright.

Soon after they docked, George arrived in a carriage, with his clothes, to take him back overland; but they'd all become such good friends that he spent the rest of the day out fishing on the *Marie-Berthe*. They caught strings of mackerel, and when they left him at the jetty again, he bought several and gave them enough money to drink his health, and more.

MACKEREL WAS NOT a super-fine fish, to be sure, but grilled with mustard and a dash of vinegar it made a good dinner for the hungry. Better than today's lunch promised to do: a heavy whiff of it came suddenly to his nostrils, and another—no, really, what a stench this was! He remembered Henri was to cook the beast on a spit over the kitchen-yard brazier; in that case, the arbor was no place to be this morning.

He went down the gravel path, keeping a handkerchief pressed under his sensitive nose. And here was George, in his shirt sleeves and country squire breeches, standing by and directing Henri at the roasting spit.

"Victory, dear fellow! He's finally got her trussed."

The half-blackened body on the spit could have been taken at first for a large hare's, with its long body. But its ribcage was deeper, and then there was the extraordinary length of its limbs. Even with the unpleasantly familiar extremities cut off, they had to be pinned clutching the pole on which they roasted.

"You realize, George, we shan't be able to eat the thing if it goes on smelling like this."

"Don't trouble yourself, the fumes will burn off. Henri assures me its insides were healthy. I suppose a longer marination might have been in order—but the whole point was to serve it today, with our little friend present."

"Well, I shall go indoors and shut the windows."

George watched him retreat. And should he follow? No, let the bard saturate his face with eau-de-cologne in peace; he'd go in himself a little later, preserving the dignity of a host. (But what dignity, he reflected sourly, was there about a fellow standing about with his belly over his trousers, supervising the roast of a miserable stinking ape?)

He had to concede that he'd reached a limit with Algernon. Really, one had put oneself out in every possible way: dearest Mimmie, herself, couldn't have made the bedroom more comfortable, thanks to Fredric, who'd also remembered to supply his favorite cognac. And the sea had given all due satisfaction. The Sadean spirit was happily still alive between them: his guest had smiled at the sign over the door, *Chaumière Dolmancé*, not to mention his appreciation of the latest erotica acquisitions. But no matter what, after a week came that absent look creeping in while one was talking, and the impatient humming under the breath.

Well, if he wanted to work, who prevented it? He had all morning to himself. After a late lunch, they walked to the beach, or on the cliffs, and as always he praised whatever Algernon cared to recite or offered him material from his own study of the Sagas for the poet to compare with Greek sources. And in the evening they got drunk on superb wine, and then they became "Georgie" and "Redgie," very easy with each other, until the cognac took over and Fredric carried Redgie upstairs.

Lunch with the dear Maupassant boy had been a success, too, on the day after the near drowning. What a good lad he was, responding immediately, running to get a boat launched, even though in the event it wasn't needed. His deference to the poet was charming, too, and his eagerness for the wildest ideas—thoroughly delightful. *En plus*, if one didn't know the de Maupasssants had noble connections, one might have taken him for a delicious butcher boy, with that crop of thick hair and outdoor complexion. On the beach, stripped, he could serve as the model for a young Greek boxer, standing against the crashing surf like a yearling bull, oh yes . . .

Altogether it was a fine idea to have Guy back today, and he'd enjoy the experiment that was planned for Nip. Neither he nor the poet liked George's Nip; no, they didn't. That bad habit of jumping up behind, which he must have got as an infant from riding his first owner's shoulders. But if Nip was kept tied up to the apple tree too long, he had the worse habit of shitting into his hand and flinging the hot mess with deadly aim at whatever victim came within reach.

It had been no use letting Redgie know about Nip's talent in the bedroom (first discovered by the good Fredric). He'd been amused by the idea of a trained wanker-monkey, but not interested, claiming exhaustion after a summer of frequenting the newest disciplinary establishment in the Grove of the Evangelist—his name for St. John's Wood. Resting, he said, from the rigors of ecstasy. Summer was over; autumn was the season of the intellect.

All the more reason, George argued, for taking seriously the study of Nip: now that they knew themselves, thanks to Darwin, to be second cousins to the apes, they should become better acquainted with their relatives. One night, pursuing this line, he'd raised somehow the question of cannibalism among men and animals. Redgie had quoted his friend Burton, to the effect that cannibalism was uniquely a human vice—that animals, given a choice, did not and would not consume their own kind.

"Very well," he'd answered. "We have a chance to put it to the test. I'll get another monkey from the dealer in Rouen, and we'll try it out on Nip."

So the plan had come about for a luncheon with skewered monkey as the *plat du jour:* an event to which Nip (usually confined to the scullery) would be invited—and, by happy chance, their young friend, Guy. The animal Fred brought from Rouen was smaller, a female, and as it was being carried into the kitchen, Henri begged if M'sieu wouldn't consider sacrificing Nip instead of this one, as Nip had a great deal more flesh on his bones.

"Do your business," he said sharply. The man was being paid extra to do the butchering, enough to keep his mouth shut into the bargain. Only a minute later there was a high squeal from the kitchen, the ringing sound of a tin basin hitting the stone floor, and cursing from Fred: George came to the doorway just in time to see his valet step back from the block with a tiny face dangling from his fingers, attempting to kick away Nip, who had gone into a frenzy of jumping and pulling at his trouser leg.

"I b'lieve, sir, he thinks he's next on the block."

"Where's his leash? Better tie him up outside."

George stayed awhile longer, to watch Henri's skilled evisceration of the monkey's body. He was delighted, when the first cut opened its abdomen, with the shapely fit of the organs inside and their shining colors, and one by one he had the cook identify the parts.

"And don't you think," he observed, "that all this looks remarkably human?"

"*Certainement,* M'sieu," the man said. "However, it's the same even with pigs; I've seen that. Everything inside is arranged much as it is with us."

"Really." George inferred a latent insolence; it would be a pleasure turning this man off when the lease expired at the end of the month—and no tip.

At a few minutes before one o'clock, Guy came over the rise and looked down on the *Chaumière Dolmancé*. Under this mild sky, set among orchards and stubble-fields, it was a vision of innocent, rustic quiet, down to the trellis of late roses against the grey stone wall. A thread of smoke rose from behind the kitchen wing—so, the experiment had begun. At the next bend, before approaching the house, he stepped off the chalky road to clean his boots with a bunch of grass. He'd been thinking over the fishing boys' stories, rumors about goings-on in the cottage. Not that he himself was menaced in any way: the Englishmen knew his family and treated him with proper courtesy. And the poet, Swinburne, was not only famous but also the nephew of a duke. Even when drunk, and outrageous in the license of his speech, his behavior was exactly—even involuntarily?—correct.

The other one, M'sieur Powell, who had first managed an introduction at the beach to Guy's mother, might be less reliable. He said he was from Wales and a gentleman scholar. The harbor talk said he had rented the cottage in order to practice deplorable vices not permitted in England. He'd brought a young boy with him when he arrived from Paris and kept him for weeks, ostensibly as keeper to that demon of an ape . . . but in reality? Then the boy disappeared— someone said he'd been seen last in Rouen, at a pawnshop.

No doubt Powell was a lover of boys; he'd felt those languishing, slow eyes on himself as he dived off the jetty at high tide; and in conversation on the promenade, he smelled a tropical perfume on those dark whiskers when Powell leaned towards him. But who cared? It was the poet who was the reason he'd come to lunch the first time, and why he was returning today. The illumination of that moment when he saw Swinburne, with his fiery hair standing out against the black wall-hangings, in the full tirade of his speech—that was an unforgettable awakening for him—and even more his indignation in defense of the abused marquis, as a martyred benefactor of the human spirit of desire—*an angelic Power*, he called him, *Obscene, blasphemous, yes! But only as God, Himself, is blasphemous in the Bible!*

How profound his exhilaration then, and then his pang of shame, recognizing how confined he had been in that bourgeois straitjacket: his mother's world. He had never had in his hands a copy of *La Nouvelle Justine*, but the poet's utterance still resonated of the heroine's cry of protest: "*Oh monsieur! vous me dîtes là des choses qui mènent à tout!*" Truly, *those* were what he required, those great obscenities which were the key to everything.

At the trellised door it was Fredric, the smiling valet with a carefully powdered sore at the corner of his mouth, who admitted him and led the way to the drawing room. There was an odor of mingled cologne and incense, and the sun striking through the French windows cast a thick dazzle out of which Powell advanced on him, offering a close handshake and an opal-colored drink in a tumbler.

"Greetings, dear boy! We're drinking apéritifs of my own invention: try one, I insist."

Guy tilted the glass, recognized as he swallowed the flavors of anise and some aromatic fruit, the heat of alcohol, and beneath that something medicinal, so strong that he thought instantly, *It's drugged—I'll be done for!*

"What is it?"

"My secret receipt, dear boy. Good though, isn't it?"

From the violet plush armchair in which he lay wilted, the poet raised a hand holding in it an empty glass, perhaps in warning. "Welcome, young man. And how is the lady mother today?"

"Quite well, I thank you." In fact, they'd been quarrelling and he'd left her going back to her bed with a headache.

"Convey my greetings to her. Mothers are everlastingly to be revered and loved." Swinburne paused, took in the skeptical silence. "George dislikes his mother. He's wrong to do so—a terrible mistake! They are the sole goddesses of our diminished age."

Powell leaned confidentially towards Guy. "Yes, but *his* mother *adores* him!"

"Sole goddesses of our . . . diminished . . . age," the poet repeated.

Guy drank no more than half his glass, but going in to lunch he felt stunned, his mouth parched. At the table he couldn't help fixing his gaze, like some frog, on a bizarre ink-and-wash hanging on the wall opposite. The painting showed a severed head lying in a scallop shell that floated on a dark ocean; the agonized face was turned up towards a moon drawn with stupidly benign features.

"So, what do you think of it?" George asked.

But the poet, refreshed by a large bowl of mulligatawny soup well curried, interrupted to save him. "What *should* he think of it, for heaven's sake? The whole thing's spoiled by that idiotic man-in-the-moon. Far better the blank disk presiding, as it does."

George, shifting in his seat at the head of the table, suppressed his irritation. "But why impose rules of realism on an allegory? Reject the moon's face and you might as well reject the entire piece."

"Yes, now that you mention it. George, get your dealer to exchange the thing."

"Well, we'll see. Nonetheless, it's an interpretation of a favorite theme of yours: the torments of embodied mind, supervised by a malign Providence. Not so?"

The poet turned to Guy. "Providence, as your great marquis observed, is an abominable phantom, a *bougre des bougres! A* shameless nothing—yet it's played inexcusable tricks in my own life. Imagine! I have a cousin, a barbaric idiot, who stands alone between myself and an earldom. I had hopes that his evident unfitness for the continuation of the line would ensure his celibacy. But no, he has recently married as big a fool as himself. I was tempted to send them as a wedding gift a Parisian *condom*—treated, moreover, with some subtle poison that would cause both of them to expire, in long and various agonies, on their wedding night. *That* would have been a superior Providence!

And he raised his napkin to his face, for Fredric had brought in a platter heaped with the disjointed remains of the monkey. The meat had shrunk while roasting into tight, mahogany-colored wads around the bone. Henri, embarrassed by the meager presentation, had basted it with *sauce forestière* and surrounded it with a display of parsleyed potatoes and onions.

"Courage!" said George, with the platter before him.
"The odor seems vastly improved. It makes a handsome dish, no?"

Fredric returned from a second trip to the kitchen with more of the sauce and a dish of yesterday's mutton cooked with peas. The claret was poured, and Nip himself was brought in.

"What do you say, gentlemen? Shall we serve Nip at table, as one of us?"

This was agreed.

"And we'll offer him his choice of meats. Some mutton, or his late relative."

The monkey, held on a short leash by Fredric, snapped his teeth in excitement at the smell and sight of food. On George's instructions he had been fed a small breakfast of fruit and bread. Now a pottery dish was set for him, with a piece of mutton on one side and an arm-joint on the other.

Nip, on his chair, was chattering in hesitation: he'd been punished often enough in the past for snatching food off tables.

"Couldn't you at least add a little sauce?" the poet suggested. "It's hardly an appetizing plate."

"Nip likes his food simple, doesn't he, Fred? So, let's begin. Help yourself, Nip!"

Still, the monkey hesitated. Fred pulled the dish closer to him, relaxed the leash, and stood back. In one neatly coordinated maneuver, Nip snatched the bone in one paw, the mutton in the other, and dived with them under the table. A burst of laughter followed.

"But is he *eating* it?"

"Fred, I'm afraid I must ask you to be our observer under the table," said George. "I'll serve."

Plates were passed and portions of monkey meat distributed to all. It proved densely fibered, with a gamy and even slightly urinous taste; while they chewed on it, Fred sent up his report.

"He's eating the mutton, sir."

"Good fellow, Nip!" said the poet.

"He's finished the mutton. Now . . . now, he's taking a bite from the monkey, sir."

"Oh shame!"

All heads ducked under the table, but Nip, caught in a crossfire of stares, sat motionless with his prize clutched to his chest.

"Damn the brute!" said George. "Well, Fred, you can fetch up the bone after five minutes, for a look."

The mutton-and-peas dish was now served and gratefully received, and the claret circulated briskly 'round the table. Then Nip reappeared and scrambled contentedly to the windowsill. Fred reached under the table, groaning, and produced for them one bone, gnawed clean to the white.

George held it up in a napkin. "There, gentlemen. I think we have grounds, now, for doubting Algernon's friend Burton and his evil opinion of his own kind. Cannibals we may be, some of us, but at least we're not alone in the habit: Nip seems to take to it quite well."

Hearing his name spoken, the monkey jumped down and ran out the door, trailing his leash.

"He's ashamed," said Guy. "He repents."

The poet, silent for some time, now spoke. "Yet, I believe I did not represent Burton's account with sufficient clarity. Cannibalism, as he either observed it first hand or compiled accounts from participants in the practice, is a rite that accompanies war between the tribes. The victors signal their triumph by eating portions of the slain, and they also digest the powers of the latter into themselves. Had we thought of it, we might have produced a better comparison by confining Nip and his relative together and observing whether rivalry arose—and a policy to seize on, murder, and consume the enemy's body. As it is, our

action resembles more the instances of contrived cannibalism found
in Greek myth, as where a child is served up to its father in vengeance.
For it was we—was it not?—who reduced Nip's cousin to the condi-
tion of food."

George, out of the corner of his eye, caught a nod of assent from
Guy and decided to concede the point.

But Swinburne was already moving on. "As for myself," he said,
"I have always accepted the cruel perversity of my own species. At
this very moment, were the tender rump of my cousin the future earl
served up to me in a fricassee, I'm sure I should thoroughly enjoy
him. Burton tells me the flesh of white men is on the salty side: I
should fancy the sauce seasoned with lemon, pepper, and a pinch of
thyme."

Fred served coffee and brandy in the black-draped withdrawing
room, on a brass-jointed traveling table. While his guests sat dis-
cussing the state of poetry in France, George paced about smoking a
cigar and enjoying what his taste had made of a rustic parlor. Between the paired candelabra on the rough-carved mantel rested two
of his favorite curios: a human cranium placed in face-to-face con-
templation with the skull of a baboon. And on a sideboard against the
adjoining wall lay another prize: a desiccated, partly contracted human hand, set in the center of a square of red velvet, which in turn
was laid over an antique brocade altar cloth.

He had bought the hand last spring from a Liverpool dealer. The
fellow knew only that it had been pawned by a sailor from a ship out
of Baltimore. A relic from slavery perhaps? It must have belonged in
life to a strong man, for even in its shrunken and peeling state, the
palm was broad and the fingers long; and an innate vigor seemed to
persist in its prominent yellow tendons and the hint of an incipient
grasp.

George had invented several histories for this object, depending
on the character of his guests, and on Guy's previous visit had given
his favorite among them: that this was the hand of a heroic parri-
cide, a man who had suffered mutilation and execution for the act of
liberating himself from the familial tyrant. As he ended his tale, he
had taken the hand in his own and touched its mummified fingers to

his lips, in homage. He had seen that Guy was moved, and they drank a toast together, to all the rebels and liberators of mankind.

Today's visit, he felt, hadn't lived up to its promise—it had not managed to recapture the spontaneous excitement, the first flush of intimacy. Those cocktails were a mistake, only made the boy tongue-tied. As for Redgie, he seemed to be passing with only brief intervals from one hangover to the next. Already his eyelids were beginning to droop, even as Guy confided his troubles—how his mother dogged him, how she persisted in wanting to see everything he wrote. But the poet was good for one more effort, raising himself erect in his chair and opening his hands in compassion.

"There it is!" he declared. "You have found the uniquely terrible burden of our generation, that our goddesses have become our read-ers—*our readers!*—and in that instant, our truths become deadly weapons. So it comes to pass that we lacerate the heart of love, which was never our target. Isn't it so?"

In the silence that followed, Swinburne's head drooped like a huge, disheveled blossom onto his chest. And Guy looked at the clock in the corner and said: "Ah! My apologies, M'sieur George, for staying so late. I must take the road back at once."

"Must you? I'm disappointed. So soon . . ." George cast about for some graceful way to secure this tenuous connection between them. He guessed that the poet would leave in a few days and that his ac-quaintance with Guy might not survive Redgie's departure. "Well then. At least take with you a memento of this visit."

He turned, and the sideboard with the mummified hand lying on it came into the center of his field of vision.

"*This* must be for you."

He folded the relic in its square of crimson velvet, and made the presentation with a formal bow. Guy held back, but he was tempted, and looking at George's face—at the mingling of arrogant insistence with abject appeal—he thought it best to accept.

An hour later, Guy reached the shaded avenue leading to his mother's house. He carried the hand under one arm and with every slight pressure felt the wicked point of the thumb against his ribs. To him it seemed that so singular a talisman must already be inscribing a new destiny on him: that of the man, he imagined, who goes beyond permitted boundaries.

"And I'll do that. I'll cross over," he promised himself. Now he came up to the kitchen door, where the cook would give him a dipper of cider and a cake. Upstairs was his mother with her eternal headache, which would release him from his dinner obligations and let him slip off on his own. The men at the harbor were talking about the new girl at Tardieu's, the young Jewess. And he had money in his pocket, passed to him secretly from his father.

Meanwhile, the poet woke up and drank several cups of China tea in succession. He was annoyed to hear about George's gift of the mummified hand. "What have you done? He's bound to take it seriously, and then where will he be?"

"I've no idea. It was a simple gesture of friendship, that's all. I meant well."

"Well, George, if you *did* commit the error of a good action, all the worse for you, of course. As the profound marquis warned, you must expect to suffer the vengeance of Heaven. *Accomplis tes Décrets, Être Suprême!*"

But when they went outside in the late afternoon to inspect the weather, all was clear. Nature smiled: the sky was a perfect blue, the fields a rough gold. So they strolled up the track to the headland and walked about on the springy turf, there contemplating the bay, which resembled a great bowl overflowing with the western light.

A Wave of the Hand

~~~

PEOPLE LIKE US, the *lower-middles* I suppose you could say, were so very modest and tactful that the hard questions might not even come to mind, let alone to words. In densely populated places, in our London as in Tokyo, it seems as if an invisible protective bloom of reticence grows around everyone but the insane; no doubt this is a necessity for social living.

Perhaps if I'd discovered all at one blow that my father Oliver was, in truth, an Olive, I might have reacted more strongly. But it never happened like that. It was more that little clues began to dribble out their meanings to me, as I passed from age fourteen to seventeen: the household consumption of sanitary pads, for instance, and Oliver's dislike of the seaside. Then, his refusal to go to our local doctor (he had a "back specialist" miles away in Hampstead—well of course, *Hampstead*, I thought later). And the realization that Joyce was much too skinny to wear the heavy corset-type garment which was hung on the clothesline every couple of weeks.

These things, along with the rare and partial bathroom or bedroom glimpse that can occur in a small house, brought the realization home to me, yet so softly that even the corollary question which then arose—*In that case, whose daughter am I?*—seemed an impertinence easier put aside.

I did put it aside.

And as I made the transit from school to college, the occasions for mulling things over continued to be expended not on matters like why Oliver seemed to have no relatives whatsoever or where I could possibly have come from, but on fond recollections of the recent past: those hard days of rationing and the times when they had to cut those worn sheets down the middle and seam them edge to edge. Also, mullings over the present: how if we were going to risk washing corduroy skirts in our new machine, hadn't we better do it inside out to reduce wear on the nap? And by the way, wasn't that first row of lettuces on the point of bolting?

I couldn't say they ever lied to me. All they did was to behave like the parents one of them, at least, wasn't. And since one's experience of one's family (so I have been instructed and, in large part, believe) is the most subjective of things, I come down finally to this position: that it's enough for me to have been the well-treated child of Oliver/Olive and Joyce, who get on comfortably with each other and have played four-handed duets on the piano in the front room every Sunday evening, faithfully, for the past twenty-some years.

Music ran in Joyce's side of the family, especially. She liked to reminisce (though Oliver discouraged it) about her mother's older sister, who with her cousin had taken their song-and-dance act on the music-hall circuit around nineteen-oh-eight, wearing top hats and tails. As she said, a classy impersonation act was well appreciated at that time, and Doris and Lilian, as the Singing Danes, got close to top billing all the way from Blackpool to the Lewisham Hippodrome. Eventually the vogue for such performers passed; Vesta Tilley was the last survival of that type, after the first war. The Singing Danes retired to the West Country—Taunton, where they kept a draper's shop.

Joyce's accent became more and more Midlands as she told stories of her Aunt Doris; and from time to time she'd take a long, affectionate pull of her cigarette, then set it on the green and gold ashtray.

"Doris was the one who went to private day school, because at that time Grandad's business was doing well. So one year, the school put on a performance of *Hamlet*. There was quite a stir locally. Hadn't been done before—girls performing Shakespeare in the parish hall, imagine! They had this teacher, it was her idea, and Doris and Lilian, they were to be Horatio and Hamlet."

Oliver got up, opened the piano bench, and began sorting the sheet music. But Joyce tapped her ash and continued.

"Your Gran used to say they *lived* those parts. Morning, noon, and night, Hamlet and Horatio. Horatio and Hamlet. The houses were only a few doors apart—they lived in each other's pockets, you might say. Even after the performance was done, they went on reciting the lines together. Your Gran was small at the time, but she remembered that."

So, I thought, maybe I did have one grandmother.

"But," Joyce looked glum, "that was about when Grandpa lost his business, the problem with drink, which is why your Gran'd never touch it. *She* only ever got her primary certificate, no private school for her. And Doris went to work in a shop."

"What about Lilian?" I asked.

"Well, she'd have left soon anyway; she was sixteen. But what happened was that Lilian's parents took the girls to the Stoke-on-Trent music hall, which gave them the idea for their act. They started practicing those old songs—'The Man Who Broke the Bank at Monte Carlo' (Gran used to do that too) and a piece called 'Down the Primrose Path' they did in close harmony. Lilian had four brothers; she was the only girl—that's how they got the idea to borrow clothes out of the boys' wardrobe, and they crept off one night and entered a talent show in Stoke-on-Trent. They did selections from the play, ending with Hamlet's death. Then a couple of songs for dessert. Brought the house down. And that was the start of the Singing Danes."

Oliver looked up from the piles of music he had out on the floor. "I don't know, what sort of life was it? Living out of a suitcase, having to put up with all those draughty halls, scruffy characters . . . ."

Joyce kept going. "And many years later, one Christmas I remember, after your Grandpa died, we got a parcel from them. A Dundee cake, wrapped up in layers and layers of greaseproof. A couple of dress lengths of material, nice woolens, and a lace collar for your Gran. And a little cut-crystal necklace for me. It's upstairs—I should pass it on to you, Beth, because I never wear it."

I looked down, not wanting to seem greedy.

But Joyce was on to something else. "And you know, Oliver, I'd never have had piano lessons if Mum hadn't thought, because of Doris, that girls ought to have music. No matter what, she kept our piano. And if I hadn't learned to play, I'd never have got that job at the Hillcrest, would I? Then I wouldn't have met you."

At that, Oliver sat back on his chubby knees, holding up an old songbook. And they were set for the evening.

After I went away to Bristol, and learned the terms of historical phases, I worked the family out this way: Doris and Lilian, with their great adventure, enjoyed a kind of heroic age; and Joyce's mother, fifteen years younger, whose husband had the breakdown and then died, not to mention her going out as a Mrs. Mop until she got crippled by arthritis, hers was the tragic age; and Joyce and Oliver/Olive in their small way were the comic age (dear Joyce in her print dresses, dear Oliver with his silver quiff, his baby-pink cheeks, his capacious trousers!). And there it ends, unless you include the academic age, which merely annotates what came before.

That's how it is: I shall always love them, but with what irreversible, dire distance I see the piecemeal world they cobbled together . . . Not long ago I read an illustrated article about an exhibit of period interiors, representing different eras and classes, from the turn of the century to the sixties. One of the pictures matched our own lounge with terrifying precision, right down to the green, frond-printed sofa set and wallpaper of flower-basketed donkeys (the very same wallpaper that Oliver must have spent hours on, matching the seams). And the curator's comment? "Well, here's typical, postwar semi-detached—oh dear! Quite dreadful, of course. Yet it has a *pathos*, too, almost endearingly without consciousness of style!"

She was right, and I could have strangled her.

The walls in my house will be painted all white, the furniture quite plain, the wood very pale. Or very dark. And I'll have an Italian kettle from the Design Centre.

Even then—to think that the grand achievement of this lineage of mine should have been a performance made out of "Down the Primrose Path" and some garbled recitation from *Hamlet*, at the Stoke-on-Trent talent show! Am I to tell that (not to mention the whole pantomime of Joyce-and-Oliver, which I must, *coûte que coûte*, go on taking seriously) to my fiancé, Eric, who has not the trace of an Erica in him and who, having been highly ranked on the Civil Service Examination list, will enter on a Treasury career next month? Oh no.

But if, as that noble spirit Bakhtin once declared, all meanings will, at some moment in time, enjoy their own homecoming festival, I wonder at what point in the future those that constitute my inheritance will have theirs? The answer to this question, however, is something which their betrayer is unlikely to guess right.

Great Teacher

~~~

The variety among the teachers was astonishing; it is the first variety one is conscious of in life. Their standing so long in front of you, exposed in all their emotions, incessantly observed, the actual focus of interest hour after hour . . . ; and then the alternation of their appearances, each one in turn appearing before you, in the same place, in the same role, with the same goal, thus eminently comparable—all those things, working together, form a very different school from the declared one, a school for the variety of human beings; and, if you take it halfway seriously, the first conscious school for the knowledge of human nature.

ELIAS CANETTI, *The Tongue Set Free*

AS FOR A GREAT TEACHER, I never had one myself, not in two decades spent as a student, first in England and then America. Once, I heard that such a rare entity *had been* at the school I attended but had left just before I arrived. Sometimes I heard of one nearby, who taught a subject that I had no authorization, or apparent capacity, to study. Thus the encounter with Miss Williams, advanced mathematics mistress in my high school (her brilliance could be inferred from her arrow-like swiftness down the corridor and the rumor that she was a Communist), was denied to me, and so was that with Edgar Wind, who taught art history at Oxford. *Stick to your lathe*, those in charge declared.

Now, after three decades of teaching at ten or more institutions, compiling a variable record of success, I think again about the effects of my own teachers on what I do, and on my lack of the supreme model. I wonder what the statistics of occurrence are for great teachers—a question reminding me of Gertrude Stein's (admittedly tendentious) inquiry into masterpieces and their rarity. Troubling questions, resistant to inquiry. Surely the plurality of models available to me could have made up for the singular lacuna; but then, how much would it count to meet most of the disciples, say, but not Christ himself?

Close, but no cigar. He's nice, but he's not Mick Jagger.

I have had moments in the classroom of high excitement and true discovery. But so did many of my teachers have their moments, even the 300-pound narcoleptic Visiting Professor; even the embittered sadist whose canon for the modern era numbered eight, short, lyric poems; even the mad Latinist obsessed with getting the foot on our necks, who found her peace, and ours, in leading a group of us through a choral adaptation of Pergolesi's *Stabat Mater*. But moments are buried under the moraine of hours, weeks, semesters. What defines those men and women for me, in retrospect, is their evident damnation—trapped in their weird rites of pious cruelty amid the dolorous neutrals of the institutional surround—all those Humanities Halls: Schaefer Hall, Seaver, Ricker, Olin, Gilman, Taper, and the rest.

As a young teacher, in therapy for classroom-panic, I calculated that with due application of intellect and compassion one might gain membership in the 80 percent competent group, plus the "moments." Aim for the status of "good enough" teacher. But if only one could rest with that! If only there weren't still, within this quest, the Quest—if only insight and truth weren't at stake . . .

Could it be that only those endowed with the capacity to be great students receive the benefit of a great teacher? That is, the true disciples, with a limitless desire for enlightenment, for a quasi-divine presence? If so, no wonder I've remained on the outside of the whole experience, held back by an ironic temperament, also by incurable suspicions of patriarchy and all cognate institutional powers. Perhaps the GT phenomenon, for someone like me, had to remain virtual rather than actual.

The closest I ever came to it was in 1957, deep in my slave-of-love period, when my fiancé (as we called them) was taking Roman history tutorials at Magdalen College, Oxford, with a man he'd begun to speak of, hesitantly, with embarrassment, as "the real thing." The fiancé, himself, had no prior exposure to this category; for this institution we were so lucky as to attend understood itself to be sufficiently great already, without confusing the issue by employing GTs.

His pupils called him Tom Brown, a nickname said to derive from his resemblance when young to the wholesome Victorian boy hero of *Tom Brown's Schooldays*. By the time I met him, those angelic curls had become a pepper-and-salt stubble; he was a thickset man in his fifties, with the overcooked complexion and belly of a hard drinker. He had written one book, a study of the late Latin writer Sidonius Apollinaris, which had secured him his fellowship; there had been no magnum opus to follow.

I might never have met Tom but for the fact that I tried to break off with the fiancé three months before Schools (those final examinations on which all one's subsequent academic career depended). Now, the fiancé was Tom Brown's best pupil of the year—so who, he asked, was this mad terrorist girl breaking up the boy's concentration on work and wrecking his chances?

"Tom wants to see you," the fiancé said.

"Oh no, I don't think so," I said.

"Oh, come on—you know you wanted to meet him. And he's read your poems in 'Isis'; he's *interested* in you."

Irresistible words, confirming the Platonic view that the teacher is always and authentically a lover whose shadow-side (who can deny it?) is the great seducer.

Up a dark stone stairway in the corner of the Magdalen cloister, the door opened into a handsome room whose ogival windows overlooked on this side the deer park, on that side an eighteenth century, colonnaded facade: the New Building. (Back in the twenties, Edward, Prince of Wales, had lived here in this very room—minus, to be sure, the welter of books and papers that I saw.) And here was Tom Brown, sitting with his chair pulled up close to that of his previous hour's pupil. The fiancé whispered that this was a star athlete, a Rowing Blue. He sat there, the image of a humbled giant, holding his essay in beefy hands, blushing down to his massive jaws, grinning, while Tom Brown shouted into his ear and whacked him on the head with a rolled newspaper at key instructional points.

"I've got to do this, sweeties," he remarked to us sideways, "because Perkins here is just a little thick! But why should he get a rotten Third, just because he's a little thick in the head? No! Damn the Examiners! *Perkins shall have his Second!*"

Once Perkins was dismissed, Tom opened a bottle of claret, poured three glasses full, and began softening me up. An easy target. He put me in a low chair, and for the twenty minutes it took to empty the bottle, he leaned on the mantelpiece and tossed over me long garlands of outrageous compliments: Ingrid Bergman's eyes, I had; Joan Crawford's legs were hardly in contention with these he saw before him, etc.

Within a week, guilt and irresolution brought me back to the fiancé's bed; and undoubtedly to secure things I received a standing invitation to Friday lunch at Tom's before the tutorial. At that time, Tom Brown was teaching fifty students, one-on-one for an hour each week. I saw the schedule on his desk. Fifty hours in session, ten hours a day, ending late at night since every tutorial overran. He slept on a cot in the adjacent bedroom, next to a keg of beer that was kept flowing if the pupil hadn't supplied a bottle of wine. An American student that year was instructed to bring a bottle of Jack Daniel's from the PX at the local air base twice a term. In return he got Tom's specially tailored approach to the demise of the Roman Republic.

"What d'you suppose George Washington was thinking of when he turned down the offer of the crown of the United States, eh sweetie? And where did he figure out that old Julius-baby went wrong? I think you know the answer to that, sweetie—let me have it next week."

If he called all the pupils "sweetie," he also bellowed at them in a grandly farcical parody of the oppressive schoolmaster. Even the pupil of the year wasn't spared.

"NO, SWEETIE, NO, NO! You've got to get inside the *head* of your Tribune of the People! Look at sweetie, here! (He waved at me.) *She'd* understand the man—*she* comes out of the Woolwich Labour Party, the organization of *Will Crooks*, she's been in the Committee Rooms! Now go away and ask *her* what Decius Brutus was thinking."

The fiancé and I worried about Tom's state of health. It was inhuman, we said, the pace he set—he was killing himself, between the drink and the pupils. For nothing was held back: the door and the bottle were always open, and the unceasing, eloquent tirade ran from morning into night.

In the last two weeks before Schools, Tom Brown compiled a three-page, numbered redaction of his original insights into crises of Roman history, bringing neglected textual references to bear on the elucidation of events. He titled this "Tom Brown's Muck" and distributed it to the pupils, promising to pay them half a crown for every item they worked into their papers. (I remember piles of the heavy coins sitting on his table in a rarely found clear space.) The fiancé worried about the Muck, judging some of it too risky given the list of examiners he'd have to pitch it to.

"It's all brilliant extrapolation from the known data, but how'll it get past those buggers like Balsdon?"

I've no memory of what happened to Perkins, but the fiancé got what he was supposed to get, as Pupil of the Year, and collected eight half-crowns. My part was done; he went off to Frankfurt to become a real scholar, and by winter we'd split up. (Much later, he became a Junior Minister in Harold Wilson's cabinet; later still, after a drunk-driving conviction, he spent some years in northern exile until he was appointed head of the London Polytechnic system, after which he rode to work in a chauffeured limousine. But enough!) Tom Brown, though, I would continue to see occasionally until I left England. If I let too much time go by, he sent me a command to come to lunch. Whenever he read a poem of mine in the literary journal, I would get a note in response. He always had some connection with writers: in the 1930s he'd been a member of the Inklings Club—that was C. S. Lewis's and J.R.R. Tolkien's "writing group," as we would now call it.

The last summer vacation I spent in that region of Middlearth, I met Tom Brown in the street and knew it was my turn to invite him to dinner. The roommate with whom I shared a Park Town apartment cooked in good bourgeoise style: Bridget had been trained by her mother, who was half French. We got cheap rabbits and pigeons, shot locally, from a stall in the market, and they were delicious, the way she braised them with onions and carrots, never mind that every third mouthful we'd be swearing and spitting out the lead pellets buried in the meat.

We got a small party together for Tom Brown, with Rosy from Sydney, Australia, and a couple of young analytic philosophers. Bridget made her *Île Flottante Pralinée* for dessert. Everyone brought a bottle, everyone performed in the semi-playful, combative style we favored. Later, as we cleared up, finishing the last of the claret, thinking about founding a salon, Bridget called me over to look—somebody'd left a large brown shoulder bag next to the couch. Inside was a powder compact, a round clamshell of gold-toned metal with a mirror inside the lid and a puff that had been used. And there was an address book, immediately identified as Tom Brown's.

"Well!" she said. "Surprise, no?"

At first I tried passing it off casually, as in effect a gesture of trust between friends. Besides, practically all the men we knew around here were queer one way or another.

"Christ, don't remind me," she said. "But *you'll* have to give it back to him, won't you, and he'll know we know."

The address book, of course.

It was an odd problem. Granted that everybody in Oxford routinely discussed who was queer, and also *how* queer (the Rector of All Souls was really flaming, and a little less so Bowra the Master of Wadham, while way up there was the old history don who hung around Park Town public lavatories from ten at night, the police being instructed to turn a blind eye)—then, why hadn't we known this about Tom all along? Why, in four years of the most intensive and ruthless gossiping, hadn't we heard even the ghost of a rumor about Tom Brown being a queen?

I took the bag 'round on Sunday afternoon, knowing Tom had a weekend place away. This was the least likely time for him to be in college. Nobody was even at the gate; it was the first sleep of the long vacation. Wallflowers in the herbaceous borders gave off a spicy scent under the hot sun. A dark archway led into the stony chill of the cloister. The door to Tom's room was ajar, but it always was. I knocked, and went in. He was sitting at the table, opening a letter.

Once he saw his bag in my hand, he came to the point faster than I could begin to explain my errand. He sat me down, poured the seasonally correct glasses of hock, and began to speak, quietly but with vehemence, of how his life had been, the misery of it: "Tom Brown," he said, "should have been a woman." The life he'd lived, since he was five years old, he wouldn't wish on his worst enemy. How he'd tried the gay route, as a young man, but it was no good, not what he wanted. His desire first and last was to be with women—as a woman. His marriage—a disaster. There'd been one son, he couldn't even tell how *that* had happened, then a second child whose father was a colleague of his—he called her "the don's daughter."

I didn't know I was crying until I felt wetness on my cheeks. Tears for Tom, but also of dismay at the impossibility of closing, now, what had been opened up. He talked, and we drank through another bottle and another. Then I was sitting on the floor, staring numbly at a patch of green carpet with Tom beside me, when he said:

"Don't you remember your poem, the poem you wrote, about Attis? I'm your Attis, you see, the one you got out of Catullus 63, who went to the dark wood. Only I never wanted to come back. Never, never wanted to come back!"

Then of course I remembered it—oh God, *that* one! What could I have thought I was doing *there*? It was a free version of that passage from Catullus, the lament of Attis, who went as a devotee to the Phrygian grove of the great goddess Cybele and performed in a ritual ecstasy his own castration; but who afterwards repented bitterly what he'd lost. She—Catullus called the mutilated Attis "she"—went down to the seashore and grieved over everything she'd lost along with manhood: her *patria*, her property, her friends, and her parents. In that order. And then the places where, as a young man, she'd had an honored place: the public forum, the gymnasium, the race track. Now she was only half a self, a slave of the Great Mother, lost in the cold wilderness. Now, now she was sorry.

"Your Attis, you see, only I never wanted to come back."

My God, I was thinking, what happened? I remembered now feeling that somehow the poem was *for me;* that its grief was, however obscurely, *my* grief. It wasn't about Tom at all. How could it have been? But now, and henceforth, it was.

"Feel this," he said, and placed my hand on his tweeded crotch. "It's soft, and that's how I want it to be. Always soft. Can you feel it?"

I did feel it.

He proposed next that we should get married. I reassured him immediately, he didn't need to go those lengths, it wasn't necessary—he was safe with Bridget and me. In whatever language we used then (now not recoverable), I said we understood gender loyalty: hadn't I, after all, lied repeatedly to keep Bridget's ex-husband from finding out where she was? No, we accepted Tom's claim on us absolutely. But he was ahead of me, faulting me for not giving him the credit for knowing that already. *That* wasn't the issue. The issue was everything that had become possible between us. As the writer of that poem, I could see (couldn't I?) the promise here, the great luck of the recognition, the understanding.

But . . . but . . . ? I couldn't, at twenty-three, even formulate the question: what kind of marriage could be made between the man whose deepest desire was to live with a woman, *as* a woman, and the woman whose unspeakable craving was to live among men, yes, *like* a man? The symmetrical faces of ambition were dazzling. Appalling. The sexual life, as I began to grasp in that moment, has also its Zabriskie Point, from which exaltation and desolation are visible as the same place.

All of a sudden I remembered something more—that, as a matter of simple, banal fact, I was already *in love* and having a passionate secret affair with a certain married man. How could I have forgotten this, even for a moment, when it was, really, the truth? To equalize the confidences between Tom and me, I confessed his name.

"Never heard of the man," he said sharply. "What does he teach?"

Now I confessed something far worse about him than his marital status: he was a Mods don, a teacher of classical literature, not history.

"GOOD GOD!" he burst out. "NO, NO, NO! That won't do, it'll never do—you can't learn anything from *him*!"

But could Tom ever have been my teacher? I'd seen him at work, how adroitly he drew out of the pupils where they came from and what that meant to them, where they'd been to school, the politics and religion of their families. And then how he used everything he knew to connect them to the Roman past, to imagine for them an intellectual future with the subject and, beyond that, a life in which all their own history and resources could come to fulfilment. It was a kind of teaching that required the face-to-face explorations that no lecture room allows; and to this day it is the only kind of which I have some understanding, in which I can give whatever I have to give. Tom Brown showed me that. Even better, by describing me to myself—not as Joan Crawford, to be sure, but as the apprentice in the Committee Rooms of the Woolwich Labour Party and as the poet who took on the voice of Catullus's mutilated hero, Attis—he showed me as nobody else had something of the nature of my stake in the world.

But when Tom read my poem, that had little to do with teaching. In the process of reading himself into it, he seemed even without intention to have evicted me from it. And then I saw he could imagine whom I might marry—the fiancé, or himself—but that was all the future he could devise for me.

I let the impasse stand.

By this time the sun was down behind the great trees flanking the colonnaded hall across the lawn; we had drunk everything in the room, and Tom Brown was due at another dinner engagement. He fetched a necktie out of his bedroom, looked at it, and stuffed it into his pocket—reluctant to put it on in front of me.

"I'm such a bloody fraud, sweetie," he said. "And oh, I am so tired of it."

From the cloister, he insisted on taking a detour via the deserted Fellows' Common Room, where he said women were never allowed to enter, and there poured us each a glass of the Fellows' sherry.

"If anybody were to find you here, I would be *most severely* disciplined by the colleagues. It's an offense, a serious offense!"

What could one say? The Magdalen sherry was a good sherry, not a doubt of it; the Fellows had themselves a nice room here, linen-fold paneling, was it? And leather chairs and some kind of oriental rug underfoot. But the weight of transgression that he so acutely felt and savored was lost on me, with the best of will and sympathy; and now that I've reached the age that Tom was then, I can't help thinking, *Ah Tom, you were truly a girl—not a woman—always a girl.*

I kissed him and held his hand tightly until we came down to the gate, and he turned left over the bridge towards the Headington Road.

After a silence of perhaps two months, Tom invited Bridget and me to meet his new friend, Maud: they were, he confided, looking for a house together. Maud had long, iron-grey braids, coiled and fastened over each ear; she wore brown corduroys and had a strong-minded, butchy look about her. She told us, with a cool smile, that Tom was giving up all that craziness and the late dinners in Hall. It was high time for him to lead a regulated life.

We'd see no more of Tom Brown: a true and perhaps a great teacher, although he was not mine.

"D'you really think," Bridget said afterwards, "living with her's going to be worth it for Tom, just so as to wear a *skirt* on the weekend?"

At that time, neither one of us thought of wearing anything but jeans. Still, although unimaginable to us as a state of things, I said I thought it must be so.

Spion Kop

~~~

HOW BRIAN ARGUED his mates into letting her join the peer group's weekly pub night, she never knew. Part of it might have been a concession to a woman from his old university, letting her be rated, say, two-thirds equivalent to a bloke? But most likely—no, certainly—it was that he'd spilled the beans about this Susan being Jim's "bit of stuff." How could he resist? Tickled to death to confide that brother Jim, the darling of the family, star graduate of St. Ignatius and then Cambridge, rising young historian, married to a good Catholic girl from back home, was finally, finally and royally, screwing up.

Susan let suspicions lie. It was so damn lonely, the temp job at the university library and living in one room in this city where Jim's brother was her only contact, waiting while Jim sorted out his new job stateside, and figuring how and when she'd manage to get over.

She didn't fit anywhere else in Brian's social world. He lived at home still, girlfriends and family took up the weekends, and there was still a question whether or how Susan could be introduced to dear old Mum, with the Sacred Heart of Jesus bleeding over the stove. Jim had only told her there was a separation between him and Peg "for the time being," and even that had made a scene: widowed Mum on her knees in her flowered apron, begging him to go to the Fathers, ask for guidance from the Fathers.

The way Jim had introduced her to Brian, asking him to look out for her, had been meant to set her up as one of the lads: "Oh, our Susan can hold her own, can't you love? Head like an iron pot. And she'll buy her rounds."

The guys tested those propositions the first Wednesday. They purposely decided to go to Yates's, where the routine was a "small white"—deadly sweet Cyprus wine—with a Bass chaser.

"Like it?" Brian asked her, deadpan, after he'd tossed back the short tumblerful and taken his pull of Bass.

Susan did the same, felt the awful chemical hit from the sweet stuff in her stomach, but kept going. "The beer's fine," she said. "I could take or leave this other."

"White Tornado, that's called. Cheapest way out of Liverpool, and faster than the bus."

She passed the test, but puked horribly later, in private. *Learn to chuck it quicker—get the finger down the old throat.*

The next week they let her in on their regular pub, a place downtown with Victorian frosted glass and special brews on tap, and now for a couple of months she joined the Wednesday ritual, starting with three to four pints, then doing halves. It was acceptable performance, though Frank and Terry could each take seven-plus pints on the trot. Different plumbing, it must be.

Nobody especially noticed the way Brian would bring up, once in a while, this cheap passage to Australia deal he'd read about, until the night he said, in typical throwaway style, that he was going. Six rounds had gone down that evening, but right off they knew he meant it.

"What about Maura, then?" Terry asked. Terry was the serious one, married already, and Maura was a cousin of his wife's; she'd been going out with Brian for the past year. Brian said Maura was the most attractive girl he knew, but there was her kid to consider, the one she'd had at age sixteen, who her Mum was bringing up while Maura lived with an aunt. Complications he didn't want.

"I told her last Sunday. Look, Maura wasn't dying to go anyway."

"D'ya ask her, though?"

Brian looked down, rubbed his hand across his forehead. "What was the point, like?"

Terry had a long drink, and turned to Susan as if he must put the case to somebody, even an outsider. "Maura used to be the real golden girl, y'know. There was some older guy at work that did it—married—we never got the name out of her. Bastard knocks her up and goes scot-free. Bloody shame."

Terry, always the first one at the bar, a blocky-built chap with dark hair greased back. Depressed, in an even-tempered way, every week he had fresh complaints to deliver about his management-trainee job at Jacob's Crackers. Nothing was ever to be done.

"So, Bri? D'ya tell our friends over at the Cap. Con. yet?" Frank worked in the same insurance firm Brian did; they called it the Capitalist Conspiracy.

"Gave 'em a month's notice a week ago. Leaving October 31st, sailing November 3rd."

That stopped them cold; Susan thought they looked as if Brian had just pissed in their beers, every single one.

"Well, bugger all!" Scotty said after a moment. "What d'you mean, keeping us in the dark? You've been a real secretive little shite about it, haven't you Bri?"

It was Scotty's place to speak up: unlike the rest of the group, he'd never been to college, which made him their social conscience. Scotty thought about taking courses in art at the Poly but was stuck in clerical for the duration.

"Well."

That would be the closest Brian would come to an apology. "Well," he continued. "Y'have to think it out by yourself, like. Not to mention breaking it to me Mum, after Jim already went off."

Frank ground his cigarette into the ashtray. "Look, we can't deny you're probably doing the right thing. Fuck-all opportunities 'round here. Forty years stuck in the same groove, collect your pension. I mean, bugger that."

It was Susan's round. She bought them all double Scotches so they could cheer up and drink to Brian's success.

"Ooh, the nice girl!" Frank said. "Marry me next weekend, love?"

A bit later she was telling them, as if she'd assumed they'd known about her all along, that it was Jim to blame, setting the bad example, going off to the States for a shitload more money. "And who knows?"

she said. "We could all be back home in two to three years, flush or broke as the case may be."

"I seriously doubt it. Can't turn back the clock." That was Scotty talking, and he took a drink and then tapped his cigarette with a finality that settled the point.

Susan glanced 'round the table and thought if she were to pick one of them to take to bed that night, it would be Scotty, acne scars regardless. The whole bunch had come up through a fighting-Irish longshoremen's neighborhood and the Draconian Jesuit school, but he was the one who seemed to have determined to take the full punishment of it—not to evade or escape anything. The last fifteen minutes till closing time she took covert looks at him, at the straight lines of his profile—forehead, black eyebrows, the short nose, the set lips. He wore a dark shirt, too, unlike the others in standard business gear. She liked that; she wore art-school style herself, in shabby black and purple.

But it was Brian who took charge and walked her to her bus stop.

"Scotty's taken, d'ya know?" he said, when they were out of earshot.

"Oh, fast thinker, there! Well, so am I, don't be thick, Brian. I'm just drunk. After you leave, I shan't be seeing any of 'em anyhow."

"Okay, okay." A harsh wind blew up from the Mersey, and they stood back in a shop window, waiting for the bus. "By the way, thanks for the Scotch. They do feel I'm letting the side down."

"Well we are, aren't we? To be honest."

"Right bastards are we, then?"

He moved 'round, put his hands against the glass on either side of her shoulders, and bent his head to kiss her. She felt an immediate current of response, knew he felt the tremor also, and put her hands inside his loose raincoat. They heard a bus slow down for the stop, ding twice, and accelerate away, while she seized him tighter, pressing his warmth and the hard-on against her belly.

"Not real, is it?" she said, freeing her head for a moment. "Just the usual."

She relied on what Jim told her about Brian's long and compulsive record with girls. Unlike Jim, whose face—like Scotty's—showed everything he'd been through, Brian had a deceptively unmarked blond sheen to him: the ice prince of Everton.

"It's always real," he said.

And after a deeper kiss, he said: "Not always so good, though. Lucky old Jim."

At that she started listening for the next bus, and when she heard it, pressed him gently away. "Here it is, have to go now."

He stood back coolly. "Well, goodnight, our Suze."

The next Wednesday, after hours, he took her up to a shebeen on Edge Lane. From the outside it was nothing but a large brick villa with blacked-out windows. To get in, he slipped a ten-shilling note through a letter box held open from inside and said his name; then a heavy man with a squashed nose opened the door. They went through to a large, cheerless back room where there was an improvised plywood bar and a scatter of small metal tables and chairs. Brian bought two Irish whiskeys. Over by a corner juke box three women in high heels stood chatting and making small hip-and-toe grinds in time to the music. Two more, in pastel sheath dresses, were dancing lazily together. The only other people in the place were some black men in a group on the far side, drinking from beer bottles.

Susan had to piss, because of all the beer earlier. The man at the bar told her upstairs, and she climbed an unexpectedly plush staircase, carpeted in purple, with crimson flocked paper on the walls. The bathroom at the top was decorated with red hearts and a bouquet of plastic flowers.

"Well," she commented to Brian on returning. "It's quite opulent up there. A brothel, you s'pose?"

"I don't know why else they'd be here." He nodded at the women. "Or those Yanks off the base."

"Ever tried it yourself?"

"What, pay for it? You must be joking."

She looked down at herself: a new idea, to compare oneself with professionals. In her dark V-neck pullover, straight skirt, thick diamond-patterned stockings, and green shoes, she could only be taken for an amateur.

"C'mon, we'll dance." Brian's style was orthodox close dancing; he had the basic quickstep moves down, in tight formation, and he took leading seriously. Possibly he might not be so out of place in insurance as he imagined? The record ended, and when Elvis doing "Now and Then There's a Fool" started up, they headed back towards the table. One of the tall Americans—but all of them were tall—cut in and asked her to dance, so she followed him into a kind of slow-motion jive, which he could apparently do with his eyes closed just as well as open. Magic.

How does he know where I am? she thought, when he let go for a moment and picked up contact on the next beat, with a dry, upward-stroking touch on her palm. Then she saw a flicker between the sleepy lids in his dark face. Darker than Harry Belafonte, he was, but not so black as the Nigerians at university. He walked her back to the table where Brian sat but didn't stay.

"Well, thank you," she said.

"Thank *you*," he corrected her.

After he moved off, Brian said, "I've seen fights in here, over girls. Those blokes carry knives, y'know."

"They do?" Her obvious unconcern made him flush slightly. "Look," she said, compensating by instinct, "I've to go home. You can come if you want. I'm going to look out for a taxi on the road."

They must have walked a mile towards town before a cab picked them up, and she got annoyed with his silence. Rude questions came to her mind. *Why are none of you lads over five-foot-six? Who stunted the growth around here? Will you go on wearing your boring clothes Down Under? Why don't you bring up the ethics of making love to your brother's woman?*

In the back of the taxi, she said, in his ear: "D'you go to bed with Maura, then?"

He looked surprised. "Well. Not as a general rule. A few times in summer, on holiday. She lives with her aunt, see, and I'm at home."

"Jesus."

Weren't there ways?

"I wouldn't worry about Maura," he said. "She'll get married eventually."

"Will she, though? You and your mates, I bet you always want virgins."

"Not invariably. Look at you and Jim."

She burst out laughing, at the irrelevance. Then she caught it that Jim had talked to his brother about her, reviewed her history no doubt—this fallen creature he was going to redeem.

"Jim's damaged goods himself," she said, "if it comes to that. Bad marriage and all."

He shut up then and they began to kiss. Once in her room, with the gas fire up and roaring, she poured two more glasses of whisky and got out a packet of chocolate wholemeal biscuits.

"Here, take off that miserable tie and have a bikkie."

Soon he tasted deliciously of chocolate and fresh liquor, and they undressed and went to bed with the fire still going. Now she saw even more the family resemblance between the brothers, in Brian's compact build and the smooth, rosy skin; seeing all that moved her to some borderline between nostalgic tears and sorry laughter. Even after a day's work and a night's drinking, he had that ready vitality she loved in Jim. And they weren't ever grim in bed, these ex-Catholics— it was all games out of school.

"Honey-pie," she said (pulling a word out of the past that she never used with Jim), and caressed his slim prick easily to a second erection. "My *Schatzilein*."

"Not yours, darlin'."

"I know that, but who cares?"

At the eight o'clock alarm, they woke up, only mildly hung over. Susan plugged in the kettle, then ran upstairs to the loo, washed her face, and fluffed her hair quickly in the mirror. The bathroom was shared with two other tenants, and anyway there was no time to bathe this morning. A quick rub with cologne must do. Back in the room, she pulled fresh underwear from the drawer. Putting on her bra, she saw four bluish fingerprints on her breast, and felt the nipples' soreness: she remembered a streak of cruelty in his lovemaking which had made her think, before she slept, *enough of this*. Was he bent on outperforming his brother, making, so to speak, his own mark on her? Too likely—and punishing her at the same time. She watched him hold his shirt up by the window, examining the collar line, then putting it on with a small frown. She'd bet his mother did his laundry every day of her life.

Over breakfast, toast and instant coffee in the kitchenette corner of the room, Brian made a point of telling her all the evenings he had booked up the next two weeks till he left for Southampton. The send-off dinner with the boys at work, the family gatherings, Maura.

"It's entirely O.K., Brian," she said. "I promised to meet a cousin in Manchester one of these weekends."

"Well, suit yourself." (What was that little turnabout for?) He lit a cigarette, checked his watch, and got up to lay a warm, smoky kiss on her. "Have to run."

But he phoned her at work after lunch. "How're you feeling, then?"

"Fairly screwed, I'd say."

"I was thinking, United are playing at home this Saturday. So if you've never seen a game, want to go?"

"O.K."

"Meet you in the Chester Arms for lunch, then. Twelve-fifteen?"

Lunch was Guinness, brown bread and butter, and plates of tiny, cold shrimp tasting of sea water. Afterwards, they took the bus out along Scotland Road. The air was still misty after a morning rain, and the slate roofs of the houses had a wet blue sheen to them. Women on the street walked from butcher's to greengrocer's to Co-op, loaded with baskets in either hand or with one hand on a pram or push-chair and the other holding bags. They wore headscarves and drab coats, reminding Susan that she'd put a headscarf on, too, which would flatten her hair, and a dirty tan raincoat. Only three months here and she was starting to look just like them.

Every corner had its pub. Brian told her a few were women's pubs, because among the older generation the women (but never his own mother) preferred to drink their port-and-lemon or whisky-and-ginger among themselves, while the men went to their own pubs for mild-and-bitter, or Scotch with a chaser when they were flush.

The bus went on through districts of brick row houses with

washed doorsteps, and now she began to see more people on the pavements again, men in cloth caps walking in the same direction as the bus. The double stream of them on each side of the road increased at each corner, gathering volume until it spilled into the roadway, and the bus changed down gears and ground them spasmodically as it slowed to a walking pace itself.

"We'll get off, the next stop," Brian told her. "Just as well walk from here."

They stepped down into the moving flood of people uniformly dressed in their drab jackets, raincoats, drab tweed caps. Often the men had a cig drooping from one side of the mouth, and made cryptic remarks out of the other. Brian pulled her over into a pub doorway while he lit up, himself. Three men beside them were arranging a bet.

As they walked on, Brian said: "Tell you, our Dad used to send me to the shop for a couple of Woodbines. Just a couple at a time. Old Jim'd give me hell when he was here. The old man wasn't allowed, with his bronchitis. I didn't have the heart to deny him, though; you could tell he wasn't going to last."

At the football ground there were boys milling about with yellow-striped rosettes to sell and men busy with slips of paper and handfuls of half-crowns.

Brian paid at the gate. "Don't mind standing room only, right?"

It wasn't a question. They were carried in the press of the crowd up flights of steps and out into a steeply pitched enclosure overlooking one end of the field. To either side beyond the barriers were the higher-priced seating sections, but here there was just a concrete floor slanting down to the wall at the bottom.

"Here's where you get the real fans." Brian indicated the crowd that already filled the lower third of the area. "It's Spion Kop, called after some hill in the Boer War where some local chaps got mashed up. So it's just for our side. Visitors, other end please."

He took them down to a spot by the side barrier. The crowd gradually packed in around them, everyone shifting about, jockeying for a better view. A tight phalanx of taller-than-average chaps began edging in front of them, and Brian shoved her ahead of him down the barrier to keep them off. One of them turned, flashed her a hard look that said *bloody foreigner*, and spat a gob of phlegm to land a calculated few inches from her shoe. Was she the only woman here? No, there was a scatter of headscarves among the crowd below, and two little dollies with chiffon tied over their hair rollers were prancing about in high heels up top.

Susan's own feet, in stockings and flats, were already freezing on the damp concrete, and it wasn't going to get better. And all she could see was two-thirds of the far half of the field and a strip, barely to the goal post, down the near side.

"Give us a cig, Brian, would you?" At least her mouth could get warm.

He lit one for her and one for himself. Now an orchestrated roar, beginning down at the front and rising through the ranks, told them the teams were running on.

"That's just the start of it, the Kop sound machine," he told her.

"Your last game for a while."

"Eh, there's always cricket, and rugby of course."

Moments into the game, cued by some inflection in the continuous roar which she didn't pick up, he came alert. Craned high to the right, where Susan couldn't see, he was tracking a pass and joining in the chorus around them. "Get the bugger—head 'im off—cripple 'im. Where's the fuckin' defense, here? Get that bugger —oh Christ . . . "

No need to ask, standing deep inside this vast, embittered, raging howl, with its feral descant of screams at the umpire. The wrong side had scored.

"See now," Brian said into her ear. "Next ten minutes is crucial. Either they hit back, or the guts'll go out of them the rest of the half."

Behind them and a little way to the right was a tiny man with scarlet ears poking out from under his cap, his chicken neck wrapped in a muffler over a frayed jacket, who'd set up a running tirade: "Put the fuckin' boot into 'em, get it in yer lazy buggers, put yer arses into it, get a sodding move on, get it up there, yer bloody sods . . . "

"What's up with him?" she asked. "He can't see a bloody thing, surely."

Brian looked. "The clairvoyance of the truly pissed. See that bulge in his pocket? That'll be his pint. He gets the drift, alright."

And he did. At the end of ten minutes, United hadn't yet scored or made a convincing try at it, and the little man was taking pulls at his flask, his voice down to a mutter: "Yer lazy twats, might's well go 'ome, bleeding waste of a Sat'day . . . " Around him the crowd, too, had sunk into a resentful mutter, till half time came and they broke ranks to go piss or find a drink. Susan could see more now of the vacant field, but even as play started up again, so did a drizzling rain.

"This is the chance," Brian told her. "Right now, or never."

The Kop crowd knew it, too, and mounted a deafening push of sound, getting one try out of the team and within minutes another. But the Wolves' goalie had no trouble saving, and the second effort drew a penalty kick (miss-kicked, at least), and after that the contest seemed to bog down in the mud, the players all slicked with wet and heavy-booted, the passes slowing down while the crowd kept up a slackening barrage of support and abuse, alternating with the possession of the ball.

Even before the end, a stream of defectors began making for the stairway, and Brian nodded to her to move.

"They'll be saving themselves now for next week. Think they can beat Preston—well, good luck with this lot! Need some fresh blood, import some Aussies."

Under the overhang shelter, she wrung out her scarf and retied it. "A trade, then—and the Aussies get you. To do what, by the way? I never asked."

"Dunno. They give you the names of some firms to contact. Money's what I have in mind: the loot."

Just inside the turnstile, there was a flurry of movement ahead: two men got a third pinned against the wall, holding him and punching with short jabs to the body, while he jerked to and fro and tried to hack them with his knees and boots. Brian grabbed her arm, hustled her on as the muffled sound of impact and gasping followed. Outside, she looked back and saw only the backs of Andy Capp heads.

"Now you've seen life as she is lived in this place," he told her. "No action in the game, so they've to make up for it themselves, like.

It's all just a bloody boring scene, when you come down to it. So, the theory goes, why don't we just get this old bugger here in the balls?"

Back at Susan's house, he borrowed a towel to dry off his hair, then took out his comb to part it and set the quiff in order.

"Why d'you make it so neat? For all you know, I might mess it up," she said.

"I'll comb it back afterwards."

"Tea, or whisky?"

"Let's have both, why not? Queen Victoria's cocktail."

Susan put on the kettle. When she came back, he was smiling at the arrangement of milk bottles she'd set under the windows, catching the drips from the ceiling crack in a half-musical sequence.

"I know," she said, aware of the rotted carpeting there and the blistered paint above. "But I'd rather keep her downstairs off my back."

She recalled a conversation with the landlady a short while ago. Mrs. S. had gone into detail about the seemingly nice girl who'd been renting on the top floor, till she left to get married. And when Mrs. S. went to the wedding, at St. Philip Neri along the street, the bride came down the aisle in white but sticking out to here.

"Seven months at least. She could have had it there at the altar! And I had no idea—*no idea!*—that such things went on in my house."

A trade-off, then: a few leaks for some discreet fornication. She made the tea, poured two shots as well, and settled on the studio couch. Brian had the armchair.

"Well, tonight," he said reflectively, "it's me Mum and the family: she's made a cake. Tomorrow it's the lads."

"Then you'll be packing for Tuesday."

"Looks like it."

He drained his cup, set it down, and came over, reaching a hand onto her breast.

"A farewell fuck, is it?"

"If you don't mind."

"Well, just this once, then."

"Better me than another—keeps it in the family."

That made her laugh, and when she took him inside her by daylight she felt suddenly fine, terrific, passing over his pretty-boy vanity, and just getting that right alignment, here, and yes, here—a matching of hunger and satisfaction.

Afterwards, getting dressed, he said: "So, would you have considered Australia instead? If the subject had come up?"

The idea had even crossed Susan's mind, disoriented the way she was—she in this limbo where Jim had left her. Only two airletters had arrived so far, and they still hadn't made a convincing plan. But this? No, it was too grotesque. She looked at Brian and saw he couldn't help playing the rival, couldn't help insisting until she gave some answer.

"Oh well," she said. "Of course, if things were different."

Susan thought of the hopeless misery she'd pulled Jim out of back then, and later the twist she hadn't expected to see, how cruel he'd been to Peg—dragging it out for so long, half-passively, half-deliberately closing one door after another against her. "It has to have been worth all that misery and guilt," she added. "You can't go back on it, d'you see?"

He looked satisfied. "Well, needless to say, this episode shall go unmentioned."

She laughed out loud: this, too, she'd considered.

"Don't make rash promises. I bet you'll tell him sooner or later."

"Look, if I say I won't, I won't." But he was blushing, and covered up by reaching for his cigarettes.

"Understand, Brian, I shan't tell him myself. To me, it's just what happened. No need to make trouble out of it."

But he'd tell, she was sure. It was his pride: since Jim had the brilliant career, Brian could at least be the great seducer, and how better to prove it? And she did care about his telling, but what was the use now? Besides, if Jim got the chance, he'd be consoling himself for her absence, because they'd both agreed on it, that nothing happening in this lost time of waiting would matter to them.

Susan picked up her glass, which still had an inch of whiskey in it. "Success to you, Brian," she said, "and happy days in Oz."

After he left, she took the cups and glasses into the kitchenette and washed them out. There was a chop for her dinner, wrapped and keeping cool on the windowsill; when she got it in, it seemed a little ripe, but not enough to throw out. She'd wash and salt it; and there were potatoes and onions to fry up.

First, though, a bath. She ran the narrow, iron-stained tub half full, threw in a jasmine bath cube from a birthday assortment, and undressed. Yet, if she smelled of anyone, it would be herself. Brian, the pristine lad, never seemed to have a smell. And he insisted on using his own condoms, she'd noticed, doubtless because he never trusted women even when they had a diaphragm ready. Lying in the water, she noticed how the marks on her breast were fading to green. Then she thought about Maura, and Jim's Peg, the ones who were officially left. Deserted. Oh, but their people rallied round like mad, in those cases—Maura in her auntie's bosom and all the cousins', Peg cosseted by her sisters and her friends from work.

As for herself, bad Susan, the "woman named" in the case, she was stuck all the way up here with nobody she could trust or talk to—skip the family entirely, of course—and that pretty much left her with phoning Anita, the insatiably curious old friend, once a week. No, she was the one having to leave the fucking *country* over all this. And seriously, who wanted to be one of those miserable Yanks, who had no Labour Party and had to put on deodorants and shave their legs, and wear white socks, and throw their weight about everywhere? Dear God, even if Jim were Marx and E. P. Thompson rolled into one, he couldn't make up for all she was going to lose: herself—right?—to be remade in some weird place. In seven years there'd be complete cell turnover. So much for some corner of a foreign field that is forever bloody U.K.

A bath getting cold, though, that was quite enough misery for now. She got out, dried herself, and went back to her room in the towel to put on different clothes, new makeup. After supper she might go down to the Crack for a drink. There was a chance someone she knew at least by sight from the library would be around, and you never knew when the occasional unhappily married man might show up. The best kind, those, and not only that: they deserved anything that happened to them.

How Aliens Think

~ ~ ~

GREEN IS THE COLOR that defines them, of course. They don't realize yet, but it's already there in the picture.

Look closely, and Susan's wearing a grass-green peridot and pearl ring on her engagement finger, for Jim, who's coming to meet her as the S.S. *Carinthia* steams into New York harbor. And Keith has on his olive checked shirt while they stand with their Fulbright group at the lower-deck rail, catching the last of the sea breeze and watching for Manhattan to appear out of the whitening August haze.

Finally, here she is, unbelievable but true: New York faintly materializing over the ruffled water, a crystalline formation rising in outline, higher and higher: pure sci-fi dream of a city.

"The door dilated," Keith declaims, making a kind of spaceman salute.

Susan has both hands tight on the rail. "So, we actually did it, we left ... "

These are not the oppressed aliens that Emma Lazarus looked for, the huddled masses yearning. They're something else, "accidentals" an ornithologist would call them. In '63, it's not yet the big wave of Eurotrash—just educated drifters blown off current by some personal disaffection.

Keith and Susan are headed for the same New England university and have made a convenient alliance. She's confessed to him, somewhere out there in the grey Atlantic, her evil habit of poaching married men, which, she insists, *is now over!* Hence the plan for Jim to get a Mexican divorce and for the two of them to reunite after this year, in Texas where he has a legitimate job. Keith has described his failed efforts to get a queer life among his native Yorkshire dales, despite the family's prominence in their banker's villa, despite a rural world in which bestiality is the only known perversion, and despite the wide-open moorland, its low stone walls and general lack of cover. *For miles and miles about, there's ne'er a bush*, he quotes bitterly—how true that is! Even at Cambridge, in all other ways a paradise, Keith felt constrained by his parents' expectations for their only son. Their presence stuck in his head so obstinately, the only hope he had was to leave the country.

Now Manhattan's closer, threatening to look like something real, made of steel-reinforced concrete as well as glass.

"Never mind," Keith says. "Look, we already *know* the language—how hard can it be?"

"Right," says Susan. "Exactly my sentiments."

Carinthia docks on the lordly Hudson side. When they've run the customs gauntlet, distant relatives of Keith claim him, for the two weeks until college starts. No Jim, though, anywhere. Susan sets to and hauls her suitcase to the taxi rank. At least she has the name of his hotel.

But, good Christ! Manhattan at ground level is one continuing assault of explosive noise and motion—insane jackhammers going at you from this side, backhoes clawing and grinding in the lot across the street, sirens in perpetual spasm. And this huge fist of heat clamps down on her—ninety-five degrees registered on a display. A news billboard says this marks a third summer of record drought and temperatures. The street simmers with radiated fire. Susan has no hat, no sunglasses. Nobody ever told her about this. In the bag clenched against her ribs she has just sixty dollars. She waits in line half an hour for a cab: time enough to suspect an irreparable mistake. Those three years' worth of absolute belief that she and Jim were each other's great love and best friend, her confidence that they would really end up together—some unknown percentage of all that is being sweated out of her, secretly evaporated away, every minute while she's standing on this yellow line.

She does find Jim, in the cool hotel lounge, still fully convinced that this was their agreement. Susan lets it pass—why not? Their room is wonderfully high up, with a view on some avenue, a shower to experiment with, and a bed for making wonderfully clean, air-conditioned love. Everything's fine again, America looking better by the minute.

Next day, Jim takes her along to an expensive lunch with the editor who's bringing out his study of Ezra Pound and Propertius. A cheerful guy, he orders an extra-fine bottle of wine; and what he really wants to do, it appears, is tell them his story of how William Empson, in Hong Kong before the war, arranged for Mrs. Empson to give him his first fuck, even leading him by hand to the marital bed, itself. A good fuck, was it? He confides, smugly, that it was an incomparable educational experience.

Another day, and Jim's leaving, authentic green card in his wallet, for the flight to Texas. Susan begs thirty dollars off him: taking money feels like a dirty thing to do, but she needs the cash. But then, the goodbye kiss she gives him feels dirty, too—the first time it's ever felt that way. Shaken, as if by one more bad omen, she goes back into the hotel lobby and calls a number written on a postcard: Lili's, on East 11th Street.

An Australian friend made the connection for her: Ed, the philosopher, who was a member along with with Lili and Germaine Greer of the Sydney Push—a group formed around the libertarian thinker John Anderson, and now scattered worldwide. Lili has since become a journalist, entertainment correspondent in the U.S. for a Sydney paper. Susan holds the battered postcard that Ed passed on to her. Sure, it says, in letters blurred by sweaty contact, August is her slow season. Ed's bloody Pom is welcome to stay.

The cab lets Susan off in front of a row of brick tenements hung with black fire escapes. There's a corner shop with fruit displayed, and she buys six peaches. Under the eleven o'clock blaze of sun, her too-thick shirt and jeans cling like wet armor on her skin. In the minutes it takes to drag her stuff to the right door and press the button, she's panting like a dog. Then, the sound of flip-flops on the staircase, and Lili, in a muu-muu with a pattern of emerald leaves, leads the way upstairs into a room where fans chatter in the windows.

Susan does a visual check and figures this is just a one-room flat. Another moment of awful doubt: what's she let herself in for now?

"*Christ,* girl, you look *fucked!*" Lili says. She reaches into the fridge for a bottle of cold, bubbly water, pours a glass, and puts it into Susan's hand. "Take this for a start."

The cooling liquid goes down, percolating into millions of grateful cells. And Susan's vaguely conscious right away of her enormous luck, here, falling into the hands of a true guide and psychopomp. Because Lili, who is technically almost her own age, has lived by luck from the day she was born, the child of Jewish refugees surviving the war in Italy somehow. She escaped the D.P. camps with her parents to Australia, and has escaped again to New York, where she's in love with the city forever. Lili owns all the keys. She knows, she always knew, how to be an alien.

The apartment is quickly decoded: Lili sleeps in the curtained alcove to the right of the door, and to the left are the fridge, stove, sink, and a hip-bath fitted ingeniously under the lift-up countertop. The toilet, down the corridor, is shared with other tenants—it's unspeakable, what can you do?—and you take the toilet roll in with you and bring it back after. About the guest bed, ready made up under the window, there: it's a good idea to tap on it several times, up and down, before getting in. That's to allow the roaches time to move out; if you pull the sheet back too suddenly, you might not like what you see. (Out of curiosity, Susan tries just that a few nights later, and a dozen roaches dash about hysterically. She feels so embarrassed for them.)

"Y'see," Lili explains, "even if you bomb the bastards, which I do once in a while, the neighbors bomb them right back."

So this is downtown America. Susan's never lived in such a density of vermin before, with roaches into everything but the freezer, the rats patrolling the alley at night, and a late-summer praying mantis living in the window box of herbs behind the sink. But she's never met, either, anyone like Lili, who makes this generous sacrifice without question, letting an absolute stranger come in to share her space. If she'd known, she'd never have dared ask. Even trying to say thanks, she stammers.

"So," Lili says, grinning, "your bloke's buggered off to Texas, eh? Typical! What d'*you* think of that?"

"Well, it was the deal he got. See, I'm buggering off to Boston for a year, that's *my* deal, while he works out this divorce. Meanwhile, I've only seventy-five dollars to last two weeks. And here's all I brought you: six peaches."

This stirs Lili's pride: she can deliver New York for that much, and give change back.

That afternoon they hit 14th Street and the sale at Gimbels, where Susan gets a loose, dark-red shirtdress, cut above the knee, for seven-fifty. Green sunglasses off the street: two-fifty. Later, with Susan wearing her cool, new *schmatte*, they take a sunset walk past Delancey Street to the East River view. Next day to Bloomingdale's, just to check out the top-price stuff for fall—and there by pure chance is Lili's friend Jeannie, the model with a spread in this month's *Vogue*, going through the racks.

Jeannie invites them into her dressing room while she tries on a couple of things. She strips down to a tiny black bra and bikini briefs, shakes out her dark hair, and coolly turns herself before the mirrors. Susan has never seen a world-class beauty up close before, and almost naked. The symmetrical line of Jeannie's body seems as if newly drawn, in one long stroke of some divine stylus—finished off with a horizontal comma at the navel. No wonder Jeannie doesn't mind them looking: she's astonishing from any angle.

"My God, the flab!" she moans, stroking her pale tan midriff. "I have to starve *five pounds* off, by September."

"Such a bitch," says Lili. "As if we weren't dying of envy already."

Jeannie laughs, and zips something on, smoothing and turning, looking at herself over her shoulder, then unzips, throws it down, and starts over. This is a lousy year, in her view: the colors are all muddy —nothing looks good except jeans anymore.

Lili takes leave with a kiss, and says "Hi" to a young man sitting alone, sulking on a bench outside.

"That's Jeannie's boyfriend—French," she tells Susan.

"Almost as pretty as her. And awfully young, isn't he?"

"I should bloody hope so! She's put in her time, y'know, with those rich old buggers when she was nineteen, twenty. Now she can afford to please herself—it's fair enough."

The next day, they ride the Staten Island ferry for a nickel, then it's to Ratner's for blintzes. At the weekend, they do Jones Beach, then a cocktail party in a fiftieth floor apartment somewhere in midtown. A thunderstorm has just passed through when they arrive, leaving tattered veils of cloud drifting past the huge windows, changing slowly from grey to lavender. Everything inside the apartment is in pale neutral, and the women wear black dresses, except Lili in her leopard-print drape and Susan in the red shift that she takes off only for sleep or to wash.

Then they're in a group, talking. Susan edges herself to where she can look out and watch the Chrysler building in the dimming light. Someone brings up the Royal Family, right in her face, so she answers, automatically: "Oh, sod the frigging royals, bloodsuckers, who gives a shit?"

Which an older fellow, whom Lili introduced as Manny, takes as a come-on. He attaches himself to her, bringing her refills of gin and tonic, tells her he's in the theater business, and spins her a long joke about a Jewish guy who makes money and goes to London for a bespoke suit, then stands in front of the tailor's mirror, draws himself up, and utters these words: *Pity we lost India!*

And Susan just does not get it. What is so damn funny—why is Manny bent over with tears of laughter in his eyes? He repeats the punchline, shaking with the hilarity of it. She understands the words, sure, *Pity we lost India*, but what the fuck is the *point*? Nobody Susan knows, or can even imagine knowing in her New Left circle, would be capable of thinking about India's independence that way. She's beginning to worry about aspects of the language here that she doesn't grasp: traps under the apparent familiarity.

But Manny's not done with her yet. He gets serious:

"You could make it here, kid, y'know that? With that mouth on you, and the accent? No, listen, I'm telling you the truth! Ya gotta fix the hair—I can recommend a guy. And those eyebrows! Gotta lose the sad-clown look, know what I mean? Do the eyebrows right, it makes all the difference. Believe me. 'Cause I think you got a lot going for you, so make the most of yourself. Know what I mean?"

Well, she appreciates his advice, yes she does. Will seriously think it over. (For this, too, is America, land of perfectibility.)

Then Lili pulls her away—they have to go, catch a ride right now: "Just forget all that. Manny doesn't know shit about you, remember? We're going down to the Village for pizza—Glen and Rob have a car."

"Guys in the black leather?"

"Sure, they're fine. They're both social workers—you never have to worry about fucking 'em, the whores give 'em free blow jobs all the time."

"I see."

Silent memo to herself: *ask Lili privately what the blow job is.* It's related, conceivably, to the graffiti she's noticed on the local subway platform: *George sucks.* Which suggests some version of the familiar, old-style *soixante-neuf*? It's best to be sure.

They park in Greenwich Village and walk a few blocks to John's Pizza. But before they arrive, Susan catches a vision across an intersection that stops her cold. It is some kind of super-human, well over six feet, and the dark-bronze face and those bare, polished biceps announce him as a black man—but he's wearing a woman's outfit that puts Lili's flamboyance to shame. A fuchsia boa winds loosely about the shoulders, shining bangles and charms hang from the neck and wrists, and that drop-dead dress is made in alternating panels of black and vivid aquamarine satin, with a short flip skirt. The final touch is a great floppy beret, blue and black check. He turns and paces aloofly along opposite them, showing off gold high-heels and black fishnets, and Jeannie herself couldn't command a more sinuous walk.

"Who is *that?*" Susan asks.

Glen answers. "Who, Marlene? She's here every weekend; it's her beat."

His indifferent tone tells much. There are aliens and non-aliens, and evidently Marlene is at home in this place, whether Glen likes it or not. But how would Keith, she wonders, himself a village boy, take this revelation?

The day before Susan leaves on the train for Boston, Lili prepares for a flight to Hollywood, where Liz Taylor and Richard Burton have scheduled a press conference.

"My God, aren't you excited?" Susan asks, impressed that Lili will meet Burton, since she remembers his performance as Coriolanus at the Old Vic, from years back: the voice, itself, and the great silences even more.

"Darlin', listen to me," Lili says, and the flat edge of her tone cuts memory down to size. "You and me don't give a fuck about Liz 'n' Richard. *These are not real people.* What this is, is a *press conference*, and maybe they'll show up, maybe not. It's just my job."

Even so, Lili spends Labor Day Monday applying beauty treatments handed down by her grandmother, in case Hollywood does show up. She whisks together a mask of yogurt, cucumber, and honey for the face; then an egg-and-lemon mix to massage into her hair. After her bath, she rests with cold herbal tea bags laid on her eyelids. By the evening, Lili's skin shines gold, with an under-tint of olive; her grey eyes resemble smoky moonstones, and her blonde hair, cut straight at the jawline, swings free like shaken silk.

Susan says it candidly: she's beautiful.

"Just the job, darlin'. Do what I can, given the limitations."

Lili gestures towards her body—short, strong, and rounded, on the Slavic model (when she goes out at night, she disciplines it with a ferocious Playtex panty-girdle). But her hands are small and exquisitely kept; and deny it as she would, she cares about that.

Susan thinks she'll remember everything about her time with Lili, but she doesn't remember the morning she left—only that the summer weather has broken, and rain is hammering the city as she catches the train north. It's understood, though, that Lili never leaves New York, except on business or for her mother in Sydney. If Susan is to stay connected, it's up to her.

KEITH AND SUSAN meet again at the International Student Center reception, over platters of bland cheese cubes ringed with Ritz crackers and grapes. They recognize not just each other but a shared mood of dreamy loss, which it turns out has the same source: they've each caught a glimpse of Greenwich Village, and lost it again. *The Village*, which is shorthand for everything: the street life, espresso bars on the corner, jazz clubs, invisible airs of incense and grass fumes rising from dim groups among the Washington Square, tree-lined alleys, and entertainers under the arch. . . .

"And then," Keith tells her in awed secrecy, "there was this *extraordinary* black man on the street, a *gorgeous* Watusi in a red tam-o-shanter and a miniskirt, no less."

"Of course—I saw him. Six foot five, in full makeup and heels, yes!"

"Oh, my God, wasn't he amazing?"

"Except that the one I saw had on a blue and black tam, dress to match."

"Is it possible there's *two* super-tall Negro transvestites out there?"

"Anything's possible," Susan says, admitting her conversion to true Village believer. "A guy I was with said her name was Marlene."

"You were introduced?"

"No, no—it's what he said."

"So, where were you staying?"

"East 11th. Kind of a dump, frankly. Every morning around six, incredible traffic noise and everything started up. Still, you could even *walk* to the Village."

"You and Jim?"

"No, no, he left. I stayed with Lili, this journalist I kind of knew."

Susan's bragging; she knows it and can't help herself, with Keith eating it up.

"I was stuck way out in Westchester," he says, grimacing. "Imagine High Wycombe, only the houses and everything inflated to double size."

The two of them have their bond now, which they'll seal by means of a disparagement of Boston and surroundings.

"Problem is," says Keith, "everything 'round here's so hopelessly *déjà vù*. Sort of like Manchester but with a river."

"Exactly. And all these other areas looking like bloody *Neasden*, only the houses are made of tarpaper and wood."

"Exactly. Susan, I should tell you, I've made a promise to myself."

Keith looks off into the far reaches of the cafeteria, over his Jello and hermit with faux cream on the side. "I'm going to live in New York. In two years' time, one way or another, that's what I'm *going to do*."

"Lucky Keith. I'd do it myself, if I had the chance."

They enroll in the same seminar on the "American Renaissance." After a brief hesitation, Susan concedes to *Moby-Dick*—the way, she says, you just have to concede to Blake; and when Keith reaches the bedroom scene with Queequeg, he gives in also. But then, Hawthorne? It becomes a game with them to recite to each other the egregiously ponderous bits:

"'It is a heavy annoyance to a writer, who endeavors to represent nature, its various attitudes and circumstances, in a reasonably correct outline and true coloring, that so much of the mean and ludicrous should be hopelessly mixed up with the purest pathos . . . '"

"Oh bloody hell, mate, get the fuck on with it! Right, here's one for you, Suze: 'This fair girl deemed herself conscious of a power—combined of beauty, high, unsullied purity, and the preservative force of womanhood—that could make her sphere impenetrable, unless betrayed by treachery within.'"

"*Preservative force?*" Susan figures. "He must mean pickled in laudanum, the ladies' favorite treat of the times. Nice reference to penetration, though. Couldn't get away with that after Freud."

But Hawthorne will never fly for them—the stuff simply reeks of selfconsciousness, a perpetual irritation—and at the same time he's so obviously *not on to himself.* That's the killer. Something of the same problem with Emerson, too, and Thoreau. There's a smell about this old New England sensibility that evokes too clearly those uninviting chapels in Midlands towns that they used to avoid by rocketing past on the train.

Weekends, Susan stays on campus, writing letters and watching the beautiful undergraduates from a lonely distance. Keith, who has money sent from home, goes into Cambridge and Boston, and comes back now and then with adventures to report. Example: when Anthony Perkins is filming something in the area and takes Keith up to his hotel room to give him a blowjob (no mystery now to Susan).

"Was it fun, then?"

"Well yes, flirting in the bar was lots of fun," says Keith. "And when we went to his room, I thought I did my bit O.K. But he seemed in a hurry to get rid of me afterwards. Rather annoying."

Susan tells him what Lili said about celebrities, by way of consolation.

There's a graduate student party at the end of the semester, where Susan gets drunk and goes to bed with a plausible guy from the American Lit. seminar who, after one straightforward routine, wakes her up in the wee hours pressing her to take it in the rear. That's what he really, really wants. But Susan puts him off, resorting to a new phrase she's learned, *not on the first date*. And she doesn't like him enough for a second date, although she's grateful for the new information. This, too, is America, liking it best in the mouth or the arse —anywhere but the obvious.

She talks about it with Keith. His predictable view is that American men are mostly queer but can't *fundamentally* admit it. Susan speculates otherwise: there's too many Catholics about the place, for one thing, and for another, the frightening level of boredom that seems endemic, and which she connects with the absence of pub life, of little cafes and shops, which connects in turn to the oversized roads and vast distances between places.

Jim comes to Boston for three days of Christmas vacation, before going on to a conference in San Francisco. They make love in their familiar, satisfying way, which is oddly disconcerting to Susan, for in a strange land, even familiar things appear subtly changed. Three weeks later she writes to him that she's missed her period.

He writes back (is he psychic all of a sudden, or extrapolating from his own private adventures in Texas?) to say, well, if she is pregnant, can she be absolutely sure that he's the father? He doesn't like to imply anything, but after those months apart, and given his scrupulosity about using a condom (even though she used a diaphragm), if there was, by chance, some *altro uomo*—well, he'd have certain feelings about that . . .

The day after Jim's letter reaches her, making her blush with a rage that can't exclude some element of guilt, Susan wakes up to find a bloodstain. The threat of pregnancy is over. O.K. So she begins composing, first in her head, then on paper, her "Dear Jim" letter. In it, she takes all the blame, grovels in self-abasement for not staying the course, and weeps for all the emotional carnage she has caused. But she's clear: it's over, it's absolutely gone. Jim's reply, by return mail, lets her off charitably—and she won't learn for another year that he has already met, down in Texas, the woman he'll soon call his Dark Lady, the great love of his life. Those two will never marry, either: that's how it is with Dark Ladies. But Jim continues to write Susan every year, and she learns from these annual letters that he marries twice more, though he begets no children. Each wife, in turn, will happen to be named Susan. But Susan is one of the five commonest names for girls in America (Mary is number one), so one can hardly make much of it.

Keith seems to be the one most troubled by the breakup.

"I thought you guys had the real thing!" he protests. "You went through all that *Sturm und Drang* to make this happen, and then, the moment marriage becomes a real possibility, you just blow it away. I am *so* disappointed in you, Susan."

"Perhaps I'm allergic to marriage. I'm sorry," Susan tells him, although she's dead tired of apologies.

"Not only that," says Keith. "You've deprived me of one of my favorite lines in English verse, remember? *'If Susan comes, can Jim be far behind?'*"

"Shut up, Keith. Don't depress me. Just because there aren't any classic poems with 'Keith' in them—and just because there's no Keith Shakespeare, Keith Wordsworth, Keith Keats!"

"Not yet, not yet—give me a little time!"

"Anyway," says Susan, "you'll at least be glad to know I've decided on my romantic future. It's all settled. I'm going to marry America, warts and all. I shall bake hermits, and brownies, and have Tupperware parties, and be a Den Mother, all for lovely America. My sweetheart."

"That was fast work," says Keith. "As for me, I'll be happy just getting screwed by lovely America . . . "

At the end of the year, Keith is worried. He has to visit his family in the U.K., and frankly, he looks so much more handsome, and more gay, than when he came over that it's a problem. He's trimmed down, playing tennis, and picked up a great tan. (Actually, Susan knows he uses a little facial bronzer, to enhance the effect.) When he goes out at night, he wears emerald-green contact lenses—a brilliant look. With his white tees and his old cricket pullover, well, he's quite something. But how is he to face the parents?

On her side, Susan has scraped up barely enough money from her TA work, and serving as an experimental subject in psychology, to keep her dorm room for the summer. She's got a part-time job transcribing dictated field notes and paper revisions for a professor in sociology, which pays her food money. So Keith persuades her to take three weeks out of that for a trip home—he'll pick up her airfare, if she'll come to Yorkshire with him and play the role of "the girl I'm seriously interested in."

"This is very weird, Keith, but if it's that important to you—"

"Well, I'm afraid it is."

"Then O.K. I know how to do these things. I was actually engaged, once—I mean, before Jim."

There will be the shake-hands greeting at the station, the cold meatloaf sandwiches from an old family recipe at lunch, the healthy walk and admiration of the scenery before tea, and the decidedly separate rooms at bedtime. Questions will be fielded adroitly—it'll be understood that Susan's family in suburban London is looking forward to meeting Keith, also, the next week (when in fact, he'll be having a hellfire time around the old haunts). At the station again, a powdery goodbye kiss on the cheek, warm smiles, and the charade is over.

"Did it work O.K.?" Susan asks him, when they meet at the pub in St. Martin's Lane. He's utterly transformed, of course, with the leather jacket and ultra jeans he'd left at a friend's.

"Thanks to you, I get a pass this time. Better give me your family stats, before I forget, so I can spin them the rest of it."

"Right. Got a notepad? Dad passed on a few years ago. Mum works in medical records, at local hospital. Two sisters, one older, one younger. Nurse and generally fucked-up rock fan, respectively."

"Ah, come on!"

"O.K., she's 'a veterinary assistant.' Likes animals, get it. But you know something else? Our grocer at home took me for a Canadian— already. It's happening."

"But not to me," says Keith. "With you, I could tell the rot was setting in when you got that blouse with a round collar."

"And now I'm talking differently. Still, what can I do? Just a porous person . . . "

IN THREE YEARS, Keith and Susan have their master's degrees and have passed their comprehensive exams: they've learned to write respectful analyses of Hawthorne and to succeed in the job market. Keith has won his dream job, right there in Manhattan, at Fordham. Never mind, he says, if there are crucifixes on the wall—forget those —he can already feel the rumble of New York streets under his soles, the wind through the high-rise canyons, the crowds and more crowds. Susan's thesis director has helped her to a place upstate, at Mount Holyoke.

"I knew it'd never happen," she says. "When I was in England, I never managed to live in London proper. Now I'm here, I'll never manage to live in New York. Stupid, stupid. And I miss seeing Lili, so much!"

The next time she gets a long weekend in the city, Susan's with her new guy, and Lili explains over the phone that she's hooked up now with a radical lesbian, which means she can't be in a social encounter of any kind with a man. The two of them meet alone one afternoon, for coffee. But it's a sad encounter, aside from some interesting gossip about Judy Collins's private life. Lili has gained more weight, and she doesn't even look as happy as her conversion had predicted. No matter how sympathetic Susan is, she's instructed that she has cast her lot with the oppressor, which means, in effect, she's damned herself. And does she intend to marry this man? Well, that could happen, eventually. It could? So there's apparently no more to say.

Two years further on, Susan sends Lili a birth announcement, out of courtesy, because Lili has sent her a change-of-address announcement. (She's moved to a better place, actually on the western fringe of the Village proper.) Susan also has moved, back to the Boston area.

Another summer, and Lili calls to say she's coming north on assignment, to interview an actress on location, and can she stay on for a couple of nights, after she's filed the story? Men, she adds, don't bother her anymore; although she's still living with a woman, it's a different woman. Lili arrives with a clear plastic tote-bag containing a toothbrush, hairbrush, a wig, and the extra black tee-shirt (but to be sure, her professional makeup kit is carried in the maximum-sized purse). This time, the connection is back: Lili greets her with a complete embrace, and needs no excuse of politeness to admire Susan's girl-child, at eighteen months a feminist's dream of untrammelled will and enjoyment.

The second night, an operatic thunderstorm rolls overhead at four A.M. Susan wakes, and comes to sit in her living room (how strange, she thinks with Lili under her roof, to find oneself a person with a living room). There, Lili joins her—Lili, was never woken by Manhattan's traffic but is genuinely scared by lightning and thunder. Susan gets them drinks, and they sit in the flickering dark while the storm passes on.

"I'm getting a new place, in the fall," Lili says suddenly. "I love women, y'know, but living together doesn't work. And to be honest, what I really do like is to be penetrated. That's what I like."

Susan thinks for a moment. "Yeah, now that you remind me, I have to agree, for myself—there's nothing like it."

"I mean, there's dildoes, and Julie uses a strap-on, so it's not a total loss that way, but it's still *plastic*—it isn't the same thing."

"It has to be penetration in the flesh—that other body, doesn't it?"

"That's the thing I want. In the end. Which reminds me ... "

And Lili goes into a long riff on the personal history of a famous rock groupie she's close to. "'So Barb,' I finally tell her, 'you are such a whore!' And she says to me, 'How can you call me that, when I haven't had *anyone* since the Tremoloes six months ago?'"

Rock music and musicians have already come to be her main passion, the subject of the book that will make her name in New York and beyond and give her almost everything she's ever wanted, but will also (as she tells it) take away her health. When Susan drives Lili to the station next day, she'll be seeing her once more only, in the exotic cave of a studio she's made for herself in the city—the place where she will die, recognized but alone, of an acute asthma attack.

KEITH, WHO'S LIVING WAY NORTH of Lili, up in the Bronx, does not have even that much luck. He writes Susan one letter from Fordham, where he's a popular teacher of what they call there British Lit., indicating that the pleasures and adventures of the city exceed his wildest dreams. "Wildest" is underlined.

Susan has lost track of time, immersed in the heroics of mothering, also the baking of hermits and brownies, the arranging of Tupperware parties, when the news comes to her by way of Joel, whom she's forgotten from graduate school, but who got her number through the alumni network. Keith is dead. He took an overdose of sleeping pills—enough to kill two people—and died two days ago. It's even worse than that, Joel tells her, because if he were not dead, he'd be facing charges of attempted murder of his roommate, whom he attacked earlier that night with a tire iron, and left with a smashed face and skull fractures, and who's still in a coma.

Keith? Not the witty boy, who wrote those poems verging even on sweetness—one of them, long lost, dedicated to Susan, herself. Keith who worried about his weight, liked being slender, and had only enough muscles to look good on the tennis court. Keith her friend. Now she remembers Joel, because he was the one who obtained a couple of tabs of acid one year, but it was Keith who insisted on cutting Susan in on the party, so they each got two-thirds of a tab. They took the acid together, with beer chasers. Forty minutes later, she decided against the experience. "This stuff is some kind of poison," she recalls saying, and recalls the sensation, too: the brain caught in some kind of brutal vise and the increasing conviction of utter helplessness.

Joel, as usual, just sat there, but Keith was positively ebullient.

"Wow!" he kept saying. "Wow, wow! This stuff is extremely different, I would say—it's got some definite zing to it! I can positively recommend this!"

Then she got up to leave.

"Hey, don't leave, Suze!" Keith said. "You aren't supposed to leave, baby, it's against the rules, we're supposed to stay together, you know . . . "

But she left anyway, walking half-blinded by the weird green glow over everything, got back to her room, and lay down for a night of dreadful imprisonment, immobilized on her back, staring at the pulsating bars of light the venetian blinds cast upward on the ceiling.

Then New York gave him all the drugs he could ever want and all the sex he'd ever craved. *I'll be happy just getting screwed by lovely America.*

DECADES LATER, Susan meets again the Jewish joke she first heard in New York, the one that ended with the line *Pity we lost India.* It is offered up at a dinner party by the French maître à penser, M. D. There are minor variations in detail along the way, but the outcome is identical—the old fellow drawing himself up in his new Bond Street suit, trying out the air of a Sahib—and produces once more a burst of general laughter, in which Susan joins.

By now, she's had much time to consider the random oddity of how things went: leaving an England stripped down to all but its territorial underwear, only to witness imperial America dissolving into corporate globalism. Susan imagines turning to Lili now, or Keith or Jim, but there's no one to count on understanding how it felt, floating absently across the world while empires foundered under them . . . On the other hand, she has this reassurance that, like her fellow professional aliens, she finally does get the punchline.

Sayings of Ernesto B.

~~~

"Your Sir Thomas More was a failure—a failure, understand? Why?
Because 'e let 'imself be trapped. Executed, understand? There's no
point in teaching the failures of history: I, myself, never wasted much
time on Thomas More."

Such passion in his mentor's voice, such a need to be heard, exacts
some approximation of a response from Terry.

"Well," he says after a moment, "I can understand that."

Ernesto sits back in his chair, appeased.

The story goes that, as a young man, Ernesto had to leave Spain in
a hurry after getting his Master's degree at Barcelona. Easy to imagine problems for a Catalan, with Franco in power: he must've learned
a hard lesson.

But let's see, Terry thinks, aside from the general wisdom aspect,
of what is all this apropos?

The reason he stopped at Ernesto's office, before the meeting upstairs, was to request funding for a second E.S.L. section next fall.
Clearly, they should offer it, since Willard Lake's been actively recruiting more students from Japan with marginal English skills.
Likewise from the Middle East, Colombia, and so on. Typically, these
are kids from rich, but somehow déclassé, families. Admissions has
tapped into some Japanese "untouchable" caste network, ineligible
apparently for home institutions. One of their exquisite girls floats
about in beaded dresses under an ankle-length lynx fur coat—that's
the kind of money they have.

As for the Latins, the crass speculation is they're from middle-management drug industry background. Better, in any case, than this year's influx of home-grown psychotics, recruited from hospital exit wards. Among these there have been eight emergency commitments so far—even the psych ward over in Laconia has registered a protest. It was Ernesto who let fall that the Latins often paid for the semester in cash, up front. They come into his office and count it out in hundred-dollar bills on the desk. The president loves it—and again, Terry can see his point, given the collection problems elsewhere, like from New York City welfare.

But with only fifteen E.S.L. spots available, the foreign kids are failing English 101 at a terrible rate. He has the figures from Carole, the chair.

"Carole is *rash*, understand?" Ernesto resumes.

Oh, now he gets it: the problem is Carole, here.

"You have to watch out in that quarter. She craves authority, so she makes impulsive decisions—like that!" He snaps his fingers in a crisp movement. "*Not* a wise person."

"Well, why don't I get the registrar's figures and check back with you?"

Terry has a sinking feeling. Nobody, not even Carole, is going to push for this. Yet it's so simple—just shifting around part-time assignments. At most, a tiny increase in cost. But the moment anyone around here mentions "cost," the shit hits.

Ernesto goes ahead to open the door, then pauses with one hand on the knob, the other beckoning him close. The Gaze locks on—another saying impends.

"The amazing thing about Howard, Terry, is this [cough]. He's always thinking two steps ahead of the faculty. Not just one. Two steps ahead."

Terry can't say it's a phenomenon he's noticed. But maybe that's the whole point: that after six months in this job he still hasn't caught on to the president's thinking-ahead powers. Assistant deans are three-quarters faculty members, by workload: *ergo*, three parts loser, one part tea-boy. And Terry's the newest among them, promoted from History (European/World), where he was hanging on to a full-time job by his fingernails. Anita, the previous assistant dean, took a sudden leave of absence last June, and Ernesto called him up.

Terry has to face it—in America, you're supposed to acquire a mentor, and for him, that's Ernesto. First, Terry thinks, because they're both hapless Euro-immigrants, here in *la Nouvelle Hampshire profonde*: living free or dying. And second, Ernesto's hope of ending twenty years of solitude at Willard Lake, which must feel to him like the entire hundred, being (as he is) only too aware of how the faculty despise him for his absolute subjection to Howard. *El padrón*: a man jumped up not so long ago from his blue-blazer slot in Admissions, by right of marriage to Our Late Founder's granddaughter, Phyllis. A strange case, that. But it raises the likelihood that Howard thought two steps ahead of Our Late Founder, Spencer Devine, and also his son Spencer II (now "Chancellor" Devine). Hm.

They join the clot of assistant deans at the top of the stairs; Ernesto knocks at Howard's door, and they enter. Ernesto sits at the right hand of the *padrón;* the rest line up on chairs against the wall.

And to be sure, Terry reflects, Howard despite that fiberglass-molded face may more closely resemble a Whole Man than the rest of them. Ernesto—well, like Terry himself, only more so—he'll always be the foreigner, with that high, despairing Mediterranean profile, the hair combed straight back. And the rest of them: everybody knows that George (M.Ed.), who runs Science/Health, was fired "for cause" from some high school down in Massachusetts; and Kathy (Ed. D.) is handicapped—and in braces—from childhood polio. Bernard (no known credentials, but he's Mr. Business Management) stands about five-two and must weigh three hundred pounds. Gary (Art and Design) has a riveting array of facial tics and, they say, survives on high-dose lithium between vacation visits to McLean's Hospital.

There's a memory hovering at the edge of Terry's mind. Of course—it was Hitler who had a personal staff notable for extreme oddities: the club-footed Goebbels, the monocular Röhm, a stone-deaf PR chief, plus the various addicts. And wasn't Hitler's all-time favorite film *Snow White and the Seven Dwarfs?*

Howard starts talking. Oh, but wait a second. He's got, yes, a *book* on his desk! Terry tips his head and reads the title. It is George Gilder's *Wealth and Poverty.*

Ernesto has raised a point, proposed something for the agenda. Howard exerts Instant Leadership and cuts him off.

"No, we can't discuss that now."

"Of course not, Howard, sure, just a suggestion——"

Howard announces that he can only stay for ten minutes of the meeting, but here's the gist: enrollment estimates he's gotten from Admissions are down fifteen per cent from February last year. Fifteen per cent! Which, along with the projected, ongoing decline in high school graduates across the Northeast region, means he's going to have to ask for faculty retrenchments, effective this June. Approximately? Fifteen percent across the board.

George, sitting across from Terry, catches his destroyed expression and purses his lips in mock commiseration, implying, *hey—it's all a farce anyway, this "Academia" biz.*

"We'll have a follow-up meeting next week, with Bob here to represent Admissions. At that time, I'll be needing your plans for achieving the, ah, fifteen percent goal."

Howard looks at his watch, has a private word with Ernesto, then leaves through the side door that only he and the Chancellor use. Terry notes he's wearing plaid trousers. Plaid? Looks like a golfing date.

There's silence in the room, until Kathy says, in a seething voice: "What's the matter—can't he stand us for even *ten minutes now?* Drops a bomb on us, like that? Then he just takes off?"

Ernesto sets a time for the next meeting, without comment, and hands 'round a sheet of announcements. They file out, thinking, Terry assumes, exactly what he's thinking: who'll have to go, who are the vulnerable?

The first name coming up from his list is the one that hurts most. Frank Larsen, whom he'd brought in on a one-year contract in History. Frank has quickly proved himself the best teacher on Terry's staff and the most active intellectual; plus he's a Vietnam vet with a wife and child. But the numbers in History 101 haven't held up. Kids want the American option, 'cause they've done it in high school already and there's less reading.

How many victims must he find? What's fifteen per cent of four-teen? He does the rough math and makes it 2.1. But since the School of Liberal Arts has the largest faculty group, Terry thinks they might be pressed to give up three. The more numbers, Howard'll say, the more fat. His own junior status doesn't help here, whereas Bernie and George have been tight with Howard for years. He'll go easy on them.

The second cut he'll need to take out of Carole's hide. English has by far the biggest department, and they can always slot in more part-timers. Who'll have to go? Well, he already knows it'll be Matt. Everyone else has an M.A. or better; Matt has only the B.A., plus state certification.

On the path skirting the frozen pond, half-swamp, that must have given Willard Lake its name, Terry recalls some remarks Carole made about Matt, when the two of them were at lunch in a corner of the cafeteria.

"Why does Matt have so many *moles* on his face? It's too *weird* for me! He has more *moles* than anybody I know! I'd run to a doctor if I had *moles* like that—you've seen the one with hairs sprouting on it, under his ear? Incidentally, I wish you could let him know he needs a stronger deodorant. *You're* a man, you could tell him. Couldn't you?"

But he couldn't. So, farewell Matt.

At the edge of the pine grove, Terry catches sight of the large boulder against which, the year before he came here, an employee from the adjacent office park leaned the hilt of a hunting-knife and, with a thrust (or two? three?), impaled himself between the ribs, to the heart. Live free and die.

Then he thinks: Matt's invested seven years in this place; moreover, his thirteen-year-old son (he's been divorced for a while) recently moved in with him. The timing could not be worse. And it's already February 1. How the hell are these poor bastards going to find jobs for next year? Terry doubts he can get even a year's extension; though as a piss-poor alternative he'll give them first crack at part-time.

Mounting the stairs of Blockwell Hall, named for Our Founder's dentist, Trustee and donor, Terry has another thought: Sociology. No college of seven hundred students needs four sociologists. Setting aside the two lifers, Mike and Wendy, there's Debra Walsh, who's

A.B.D. and probably dates from before the mysterious institutional convulsion in which tenure was abolished. And the junior man, Mark Price, a recent Ph.D. like himself. He gets on with Mark, but he also figures Mark is a born survivor.

The offices—except for English, which has its own cluster in the basement with the Language Lab—are a warren of under-constructed modules inside a long attic space. Mark's office is next to Terry's, and passing it he sees those extra-large feet through the opening at the partition base. The door's open.

"Hi there," Mark says.

Terry leans cautiously on the doorway's edge. The man is genuinely bright, no question, and he does wear interesting socks—jade green, pastel Argyles—that even connect with some shade in the outfit he's wearing that day. In fact, Mark has better style than anybody in the drab halls of Liberal Arts, except for the divinely slim Donna —She of the Raven Ringlets, the Velvet Leggings, and Supple, Thigh-High boots!—their incomparable part-timer in English who, passing him in the corridor, inspires the ten o'clock erection he treasures behind his briefcase every Tuesday and Thursday.

But he's never had a conversation with Mark that didn't turn conspiratorial within seconds.

"Tough meeting, I'll bet?"

"Well, that time of year. Goddamn enrollment stats."

"Down?"

"What else? But they don't take into account that we always pick up a bunch of rejects after May first."

Mark, stretching and clasping his hands behind his head, swivels his chair. "You know, Terry, I get the feeling Frank Larsen isn't someone who's liked much around here. Maybe a little arrogant? Debra, also—she's got a knack of antagonizing people."

"You think? Well, they both do a good job for us." Terry checks his watch. "But I gotta go prep a class."

Mark bestows on him an understanding smile. "See ya."

"There's an old Spanish saying, Terry: God throttles us, but 'e doesn't— quite—kill us."

Ernesto clasps one hand to his throat and, with a small jerk upward of his chin, evokes that native Iberian tradition, the garrotte.

Decode: this is meant to reassure Terry before they go up to the staff cuts meeting. Assistant deans have been warned to say not a word to their faculty, but Terry's gone ahead and prepared Carole, hoping she's passed the word to Matt; he, himself, has told Frank Larsen that he'd better start sending out his C.V. It's shameful to delay notice this late, when the main hiring for next year is already over.

What Frank said: "Look, thanks for letting me know in person. Doesn't always happen. I appreciate that."

Good God, how else?

They file in. Howard, with his usual dispatch, has his pen already poised over the faculty roster. He wants names, and calls on Terry first. Bad sign.

"Well, Howard," says Terry, "I'm sure you've seen the figures. There's some weakness in History, and I guess we'll have to lose Frank Larsen, although he's one of our best."

Howard looks down, scans the list, and draws a firm horizontal line.

"O.K., Larsen. And?"

Terry states the case for letting Matt go from English, but makes a point of mentioning his years of service, his new status as a single father. Hell, they're guys, Howard and Ernesto; let them face this.

Ernesto speaks up. "It's a sensitive issue, Howard. Matt has a *fine* record with us, a *good* record."

"Sure. But the priority is, we're responsible for the fiscal health of the college." He turns his palms out towards them: see how empty they are? "O.K., now, what about Sociology?"

Terry, of course, has looked at those numbers, and they're just about borderline.

"O.K. I'm assuming Wendy and Mike and Deb all have tenure. On the other hand, Mark Price has the credentials we need, the doctorate."

Howard calls in Ginnie from the desk outside; she brings with her a heady waft of perfume, along with the drama of a gold-buttoned red suit that puts Kathy's drab jumper to shame.

"Does Debra Walsh have tenure, Ginnie?"

While Ginnie looks up the file, Terry states that Deb, with her A.B.D. status, is far more qualified than either Wendy or Mike, with their doubtful M.Eds. No comment from Howard.

Ginnie puts her head in. "Deb Walsh does not have tenure."

"So that's an option," Howard says, scanning the list and drawing another line.

By the time he gets through, Terry is given to understand that he must submit a list of three cuts to Ernesto, with a suggested fourth name, on Friday morning. *Four* cuts out of fourteen full-time faculty? That's not 15 percent, that's—he jots down figures on a pad—*over 25 percent.* A fucking massacre! Immediately, he starts the rebuttal memo in his head. One, a reminder *re* the original 15 percent. Two, insistence on reconsidering Deb Walsh's case, given that accreditation comes up next fall, and credentials are an issue. And three, the problem of pushing the ratio of part-timers to full-timers above 50 percent (see Regents' guidelines, as if Howard cared). Copies to Ernesto and Howard.

Late the next afternoon, Matt's in Terry's office to hear the bad news. It's true, a persistent odor does accompany him, as of a shirt worn a few days too long, a suit that's gone a couple of seasons without dry-cleaning. Terry looks him in the face, says that unless they can find a way to persuade Howard to fund one more year, June will be his last paycheck. And Matt is so utterly shocked and furious— clearly Carole never gave him a hint—that he takes a couple of heavy breaths before speaking.

"O.K. So, you wanna tell me why *I, personally*, got the short end here? I mean, what's the *process*? In what way is this *fair*?"

He looks 'round Terry's barren cubicle, clearly a hard place to hide secrets.

"I'm not saying—" Terry begins. But Matt breaks in.

"You know what I'm dealing with! I got my *son* with me, I had to rent a bigger place—*Jesus!* This is unbelievable: I'm going in to speak to Ernesto, first thing."

Terry says that's fine, he'll be happy to support anything that can be worked out here. And they repeat that routine a few more times.

Matt finally stands up. "Man, you've got some fucking nerve laying this on me! I've been here *seven years*—and you've been what, *two*?"

After he's gone, Terry stuffs papers in his Land's End briefcase, grabs his parka. And hears a movement from the office next door.

"Guess you heard," he says, pushing Mark's door half open.

Mark has that confidential smile on his face. "Yeah, well. Kind of obvious if I got up and left in the middle. That was harsh, though. Having to do that."

"Howard's pushing us."

"Yeah, I heard. But hey, aren't you *really glad* not to be on the receiving end of all this?"

"You know, we 'ave a saying, Terry. Approximately, in English: 'E thinks if 'e is well in with God, to Hell with all the saints!"

Ernesto, all the way to lunch and back, has been churning over his feelings of outrage—at Mark, who's done a neat end run around him and up Howard's arse-hole (as they used to say back home) like a rat up a drainpipe. Mark prepared his move, and he's made it.

There were clues, Terry remembers now: Mark following Howard around, with that duck-footed little hustle of his; Mark asking Ginnie what Howard's schedule looked like for that afternoon; Mark popping his head in while a meeting was going on in Howard's office. What was it he said? That he had a draft of something. Draft of what?

Now the word's out: Howard and Mark have cooked up an idea together for a new master's degree in social and public services. The Social and Public Services Program—hereinafter to be known as "SPS." The genius of it is that it can use existing faculty resources in Social Science, Business, and Health: thus, recruiting can start next year even while the accreditation request goes in. And of course, though no one's been named, Mark is poised to become its director.

Ernesto collapses into his office chair. His face has darkened to an ominous purplish-grey, his expression constricted with anguish. He takes a bottle of Maalox from his desk and pours straight from it down his throat. Terry tries to leave, but he gestures: no. Chronic gastritis, he explains—wait a moment and it'll pass.

"You know," Ernesto says, after a quietly massive belch, "I must admit I was *not* impressed with Mark, the way he behaved in this crisis. Running to Howard, 'iding be'ind the skirts. Special dispensation, understand? Well, it's been quite an insight, this past week."

He pauses, puts his hand over his mouth again. "Letters are going out tomorrow. You spoke to Larsen, and Matt?"

Terry confirms, adding that given the plans for the new program, he assumes Debra's case is being reconsidered: they'll need her to develop courses.

Ernesto, distracted, says "Possibly, possibly." Then he bursts out with what's really on his mind, a tirade against Howard and this project that Mark's sold him on.

"Howard's like a child with a new toy, a *child*, understand? But this is where 'e gets into trouble: 'e doesn't realize that outside these walls, *nobody* cares what 'e thinks. This idea, it's a joke, nothing but a made-up piece of air!"

And he blames Mark, who's been persuading Howard towards this fantasy of an alchemical marriage between the academy and the marketplace—at which he, Howard, will be the priest and Mark the best man. Then (and this, Terry sees, is the knife to Ernesto's heart), if the match goes through, Mark will leap right over him and become Willard Lake's first graduate dean.

A coup, indeed.

Carole hears about the SPS graduate program plan, and asks Terry who's going to head it.

"Well, and this is unofficial, in confidence, but it'll have to be Mark Price."

"Then I don't mind telling you, a lot of people are going to be very unhappy about that. See, I *know* Mark—I have a brother in *precisely* that mold. Completely out for himself, could care less about anyone else, just screw 'em!"

While she's talking, Terry clicks that this is a perfect echo of the way he's heard Matt talk about Carole: "That woman is *exactly* like my ex-wife—completely focused on her own nutty version of reality. You can*not talk* to these people!"

So it's even with relief that, at the end of the day, he finds Mark sitting in his next-door office kicking back with a can of diet soda, openly contented with the world.

"Congratulations," Terry says in all sincerity. "Good call, there."

"Thanks, Terry. I know there's a lot of people thinking, this thing is just about Mark Price. But Howard's right on this: without endowment, we've gotta go the entrepreneurial route. Simple."

Terry, thinking out loud, says isn't Howard going to have to commit some resources to this? Seed money? They'll obviously apply for grants, but that takes time.

Mark takes a pocket inhaler out and sniffs deeply once, twice. "Well that's gonna be our problem. Howard wants this thing *now*, read 'yesterday.' But he doesn't want to commit the resources, money, to it in advance."

Meanwhile, it's already March, and Kathy's poodle has showed up with a green dye-job for St. Patrick's Day. Biodegradable color, she assures everyone. Doesn't hurt Baby a bit.

"It's an old saying by a shrewd man, Terry: Faced with the choice of dealing with a fool or a knave, I would choose the knave. For the knave sometimes takes a rest from being a knave. But a fool's a fool twenty-four hours a day. There you have it."

Ernesto has Terry's latest memo in front of him. This is apparently the usual kind of mess that hits as the spring semester winds down. A couple of cute young work-study students, assigned to the enclave outside the president's office, have complained up there about these "insulting" D grades Carole's given them on their English papers. And Kevin, the *padrón*'s golf partner, the man who never lets Howard's coat hit the floor, has laid a couple of the papers on Terry. Lets it be known that Howard wants this looked into immediately as a potential grievance. Subtext, bring Carole into line here.

Terry knows one of the kids from class: Stacie, currently flaunting a white, see-through and plunging blouse, black mini, fishnet stockings, and heels. One of these little gal pals Howard and Kevin pick up for themselves occasionally. He's kept his official cool and leafed through the two essays: "Why Abortion is Wrong" and "Protecting Our Enviroment" [sic]. Carole has scrawled *Development?, Supporting details?, Address the opposition?* in the margins. Fair enough. At best, he could see giving them a C–, but Carole's given these kids her time and attention for months now, and patience does run out.

He'd like to bury the matter—that key move in an administrator's repertoire of moves—but Kevin has kept calling. So he's met with Carole: *O.K., take care, and keep communications with these kids open.* Then the memo to Kevin, copy to Ernesto, putting the discussion on record.

"The problem, Terry," says Ernesto, "is that you never know if Kevin's really acting as Howard's agent or not. Sometimes 'e's taking the bit between 'is teeth. I say no more, you catch my drift."

Whatever, Terry thinks. Who gives a shit?

"Kevin is not . . . cerebral, understand? That man sees what 'e wants to see."

Next day, Kevin's on the phone saying he appreciates Terry's efforts to follow due process, but "Howard still thinks something has to be done." About Carole.

Terry puts down the phone, having stonewalled politely but unmistakably. If Howard wants to harass or fire Carole, let him do it himself, openly. He'll have no part of it. But she won't be fired. Why? Because Howard won't want to pay any more unemployment money this year.

Then it comes to Terry, what just happened. He has personally failed the test of absolute loyalty. *Failed, understand?*

Deb Walsh stops by to mention that she has a hysterectomy date set for late May and will have to miss Commencement. And recalls— at random, it seems—the fact that Howard, eleven years ago, took one of her evening classes in Psychology here.

"He did?"

"Absolutely. He was in Admissions then. A good-looking guy— well, he still is, of course."

Good-looking. Has she still *no idea* Howard's been trying to get her riffed, in spite of what he's leaked to Carole on that score?

"You remember what grade you gave him?"

"Oddly enough, yes. B+, it was."

Well, that'd do it.

At afternoon's end Terry drops again into Mark's office, for this is the hour when a knave may take a rest from his knavery. He finds the man in a rare troubled mood, popping Tylenol and taking out his nasal spray frequently for a snort. In front of him is the draft of Howard's official SPS proposal document. Mark kicks the door shut.

"Howard's vocabulary isn't, well, all it might be at times," he says. "See, here he's got 'enjoined' where he probably needs something like '*con*joined.' And this last section he's titled 'Epiphany'—that can't be what he means."

"'Epitome,' maybe?"

"Well, I already gave him three pages of revisions I thought were important to make. And Ginnie sent the word down: no changes on this. Point is, if it has to go through the Regents, and then the accreditation team . . . "

Terry has to feel for the man. Yet, at the next meeting of Howard with Ernesto and the assistant deans, here's Mark tickled pink as his Oxford shirt, playing the new "His Master's Voice" as he briefs them all.

"So the schedule Howard wants us to meet goes this way . . . As Howard's expressed to me, on that . . . "

He leans forward while he's speaking, head tilted a little sideways towards the *padrón*, so his glance comes up at them almost coyly.

Then Terry looks over at Ernesto, casually, and is so shocked by what he sees, he wants to call out *Stop, for God's sake—the man is ill!* It's not just the insistent tremor working in Ernesto's jaw, not just the dangerous flush under the skin, but his eyes, bloodshot and forced wide open, as if from some inward pressure. Terry's convinced that he's looking into the face of a man at imminent risk of collapse.

He does nothing. Because what does one do? The meeting ends; Ernesto rises and walks from the room with the stiff gait of a Nosferatu. Terry ought to follow him, take his arm, say something, say *Ernesto, save yourself!* But he has to catch Howard, first, about the still-pending Deb Walsh case.

Briefly he runs his argument to Howard—that Deb's needed for the SPS courses next year; and meanwhile, the delay in deciding about her contract means that, professionally speaking, they must give her a year's grace to find something else.

Howard acts surprised. Says he thought Terry would've notified Debra Walsh a while back that she might not be renewed. And surely, given Terry's excellent rapport with Mark, he knew Mark did not see her as fitting into the SPS program teaching group.

"But Deb wasn't sent the letter that Frank and Matt were?"

"I'm not sure. You better check with Ernesto, or Debra."

He calls Debra the same night; she's heard nothing. She listens for a minute, then erupts in a blast of rage, disbelief, utter contempt. Who the *hell* does he think he is, coming in out of nowhere and wrecking everything she's built up in that goddamn place? When she's through, and he's said that he understands her reaction entirely, she adds: "You may as well know, I'm not going to take this lying down. I know it's Mark at the bottom of this. And I'll be in Howard's office first thing tomorrow morning."

Terry says he'd be very happy to go in with her.

"Howard knows my views. And the college at least owes you another year."

"And *I'm* telling *you, that's* not good enough, either!"

He'll never know what went on in Howard's office the next morning, but Mark stops by at five o'clock to say there's been a turnaround, and Deb Walsh will be teaching one more year. Not his preference, he says, and Howard detests the woman too; but there were some kind of legal threats.

The look he directs at Terry includes a shade of distant compassion: something new.

"The carriage of civilization rolled through Europe, and left its dust in Spain."

In late May, Ernesto is attempting a philosophical view of things. America is, after all, the land of potential. He reflects on the slow but unmistakable progress that Willard Lake is making, of which Terry's presence is one token. Even Kevin, he says, concedes that Terry is "a class person."

Well thanks, Kevin. They walk together past the flowering lindens and the lilac bushes to Ernesto's office. Once there, he finds a letter open on his desk, gives a short sigh, and pushes it across to Terry.

"Oh yes," he says. "Maybe this could be a nice little course to offer, in intersession?"

The time is after lunch, so he reaches in his drawer for the Maalox. And Ernesto has developed, Terry noticed while they walked, a perceptible listing to the left side: it's best these days to stay on his right hand.

The letter's on crested notepaper; it's from a state legislator in the local district, the Rt. Hon. William O'Malley.

DEAR DEAN,

It was a pleasure meeting you, courtesy of my very good friend President White.

Following our discussion, the course I have chosen to teach in fall semester is The Politics of Participation. I append a short syllabus. I look forward highly to this opportunity . . .

Yours, etc.

The syllabus is a half-page affair—no bibliography, of course. Ernesto makes a deprecatory gesture.

"A good friend of Howard's, did a few favors for us, I gather. We 'ad lunch, last week."

Terry's not going to make this easier.

"I know," says Ernesto, "it's unorthodox, but if you can find somewhere in the schedule . . . "

"Does he have a C.V.?"

"Of course, of course, 'e sent a full résumé. Ginnie must 'ave it upstairs."

He phones, and waits while she goes looking. "No?" He puts down the phone. "I'm afraid Ginnie doesn't yet 'ave the résumé."

"Also, I wonder if he knows how much we pay: just over a thousand for the semester?"

"Perhaps, Terry, you might write to him, give him those details, when you've looked at the schedule."

God throttles us, but He doesn't quite kill us.

Doesn't he, though, Terry thinks when he visits Ernesto in his hospital bed at home in late August.

Ever the professional, Ernesto waited until after Commencement before having the first of a series of strokes. Now he lies quietly, and after his devoted wife takes the bunch of flowers from Terry, he turns his eyes and lifts his one usable hand, opening it in one of his small, eloquent gestures, as if to say, "*This* is what I've come to."

Trapped. Executed, understand?
"Everyone," says Terry, "feels it's not the same place without you. We really need you back, Ernesto."

He frowns slightly. "No, Terry, don't speak of it."

Yet what else have they to talk about? Terry doesn't know, and can't recall afterwards. Only that at a certain moment, Ernesto reaches out to him and says: "Something you should remember."

One more time the Gaze takes hold:

"If there's anything you need, Terry, anything at all, go to Howard, and ask 'im. Don't bother with those nobodies. Go to Howard 'imself, and just ask, understand?"

"I understand, Ernesto. Thank you."

He grasps the hand with all the feeling he can muster, knowing that there's not a chance he'll ever bring himself to ask a favor of *el padrón*. Not in this world: the world from which Ernesto is delivered, in October, by a final, decisive stroke.

The Monday after his memorial service, Ernesto's secretary calls Terry and says it was his particular wish that the desk in his office be transferred to Blockwell Hall, for Terry's own use. Later that week— astoundingly, considering the heavy steel frame of the thing—a maintenance crew hauls it up to the landing outside the row of cubicles for History and Sociology. But the corridor between the partitions is too narrow to allow it to come any closer to Terry's office. He tries this angle and that; nothing works.

For a long time it stays where it is, a ledge for students to sit on, have a soda, and swing their heels, waiting for some elusive instructor to show up. Eventually, Terry notices it has migrated into a third-floor classroom where, as it happens, he's never taught a class.

Death of the Mother

~~~

IT IS, together with the death of the father, among the most common themes in short stories submitted to editors of literary journals. Easy to imagine, then, the miasma of tedium and revulsion clouding the piled-high office, after four or five such in a morning:

"Got anything there?"

"Another mom bites the dust."

"So what else is new?"

"Folks certainly have their gall, do they not? You wonder if they even got the poor woman's headstone up, yet."

"Need help financing it, maybe?"

Raucous mirth, such as must humanly relieve the manuscript-infested scene.

"Try *The New Yorker*, sucker!"

"What she die of, this time?"

"Let's see here. Mixed feelings of narrator, check. Sad unfulfilled life of mom, check. No, I don't see anything."

"Negative autopsy results? Hell, forget it."

"Back on the heap, then. I dunno—*fuck*—it's all *dogshit* today."

So it goes, they say, in the editorial offices.

Meanwhile, the author pleads guilty as charged: *mea culpa, mea culpa, mea maxima culpa!* But that was a dozen years ago, and those unpublished words, on the now unreadable diskette with its outdated software, have degraded like the litter of clay scraps in a studio which the sculptor pounds back into the mix.

Jonathan Swift long ago declared the meaning of the mother's death for her grown child. Hearing the news of it for himself, he wrote: *The last Barrier between Myself and Death has fallen.*

A mother's protective task ends with her remaining alive until the children have taken secure root in the world. My own—ours—performed that duty with the same fortitude she'd brought to maternity from the start: a young woman not, by her own account, gifted in handling small children but determined to honor her obligations better than her own parents had.

Which she did, throughout the privations of the war years and after. In our house, beatings were uncommon enough to be separately remembered disasters, ending in tears and headaches all round. By contrast, the grandparents had lived a genially selfish, hand-to-mouth life of the senses, firmly slapping down any head that bobbed over the threshold of notice, and dealing out thrashings and kindnesses (for they played favorites, too) as the mood or the drink took them. She, however, imposed on herself a sacrificial discipline, fighting her own impatience, putting our interests first, although her own immense needs cried for attention.

And she was poorly rewarded, after all—who could deny it?—when both her daughters ran off to marry total strangers in foreign parts. To compound that, after nursing one husband through his last illness (the lung cancer) and getting one more chance at the safe haven of marriage, she found herself, after a few years of contentment, bearing the same burden again, as her second husband became fatally ill (the liver cancer).

It couldn't have been more than a year after the death of our stepfather that she herself (unspeakable fate!) developed an ovarian tumor, rapidly invasive; and from the diagnosis in February until the end in December, she woke daily at first light to the same dire story. Got up, and saw it repeated back to her in the mirror by the greyish cast of her skin, knowing that her own red blood was being secretly diverted to nourish the greedy *faux* fetus below.

On the dressing table facing her bed were two photographs: one showed her older daughter, the gifted teenage violinist, joyously hugging her instrument case; and the second was taken at her son's wedding, equally joyous—his miraculous bride in a white cascade of flowers, tulle, and satin, against the polluted urban brick of the church. There was her happiness. (No image of her middle child, *et pour cause:* for if a daughter can be said to have seduced and abandoned a mother, then that was my primal offense.)

It was my sister, her first-loved, who brought her to the hospital for the last time. The barrier of her diaphragm had been pierced from below, and she was coughing blood from the lungs. There in the lobby she passed into the hands of a nurse, was taken to a curtained bed in the ward, and, as the needleful of morphine was gently pumped and withdrawn, she died.

The day before, I heard her voice on the transatlantic telephone. The call came while I was cooking supper; I wiped my hands on a green pinafore (her gift) before picking up. She said, with that awkward, time-delayed effect of the early satellite transmissions, "Goodbye . . . dear. Love to you, and . . . the children."

"I'll come over, O.K.? I'll get on a plane tomorrow or the next day —see you soon—lots of love till then!"

I put the phone down, and seeing the children were troubled (or embarrassed?) by my disordered face, pulled the green pinafore up to hide it.

Early next morning, my sister called to say she had died.

The date was so near Christmas that her cremation couldn't be organized until January 2nd: the funeral company staff were on holiday. Before New Year's Eve, I caught a standby flight out of icebound Massachusetts and landed in Gatwick at dawn. How gentle the air was, and how misty green the fields, driving south to Bexhill over the Downs with my generous brother, under a sky marbled in pastels.

The funeral directors had put her body in cold storage in their Hastings facility. At the office I asked if I could see her, but the man who handed over the paper packet with her two rings (emerald-set engagement ring from her first marriage, wedding ring from her second) discouraged it. The point was, with cremation there'd been no embalming. This was the frugal way we did things in our family. *She would not*, he said softly, *be well to look upon.*

And which of us would, after ten days in the fridge?

I accepted his judgment and went on to stay at my mother's bungalow, which retained more of her presence surely than her body did.
She'd arranged everything here: the aura of Nivea Creme and Fairy
Liquid, Jeyes' Fluid in the bathroom, the breakfast cups on hooks in
the dresser, the upending of the dish mop in a jar behind the draining
board. Currents of warm air eddying through the rooms felt like breath
on the face and hands. When I took out her last three bacon rashers
and cut them up to throw to the waiting birds, I felt myself enacting
her own movements, even her precise stance at the chopping board.

Seduced.

She'd fallen into my twelve-year-old hands, ready and waiting,
because it's true I always wanted her to love me more than she could;
and once she realized that I'd noticed her misery and would do anything to lighten it and bring her closer, she finally gave way and let it
spill, poured it all into me. From then on, I would never be able to
distinguish between the beloved person she was and the staggering
weight of her sorrow.

There were things gone wrong from the start, she told me. She
thought, in retrospect, that she married our Dad mostly because she'd
had sex with him. He married her, she thought, mostly because his
mother had died about that same time. She changed her first given
name, Queenie, to her third name, Mary, which was also (*Wait, don't
do it!*) his mother's name. When she was pregnant with her third
child, he told her he wasn't cut out for marriage. But he didn't leave
her, because, well, because. He took revenge by mistreating his
youngest, his son, and he wouldn't talk to a marriage counselor—
wouldn't talk, period. Now nothing was going to change.

On first hearing that sentence from her, I couldn't really believe
it. But then, I was reading *Anna Karenina* at the time and couldn't for
the life of me figure why these characters felt so direly compelled to
do the things they did. When I finally grasped her point, the reality
that *nothing was going to change*, this intoxicating privilege of being
in the charmed circle of her confidence suddenly turned sour, became
something too awful to bear.

Did I promise that one day I'd take her away from all that? To my
shame, it's very likely.

But what's certain is that I began plotting my own escape. In the privacy of the bedroom, while my sister was out dating, I set down on a sheet of paper, first, that I was no longer a Christian believer but a convinced materialist; and, second, my vow that I would either get out of England at the age of twenty-one or commit suicide. Put the sheet of paper in an envelope, sealed it with sealing-wax, went downstairs and made my incurious father sign his name on the outside of the envelope, with the date.

Done.

I did at least leave home on schedule, which seemed enough reason (along with sexual interests) to postpone suicide a little while longer. Then, in 1961, I took ship at Southampton, with my mother standing witness on the dock.

And abandoned.

Now I spoke to her favorite robin on the buddleia bush, and to the starlings in the pear tree and along the fence: "Make the most of it; after Sunday there'll be nobody here."

They didn't fly down immediately, as they would have for her, but sat perched there until I went inside.

It was time for me to put on raincoat and scarf, and carry out my plan for lunch at the Red Lion pub in Hooe: a three-mile walk by the fields. The previous spring when I visited, my mother and I had started in that direction, but it was too far for her, and we kept to a smaller circuit in the neighborhood. But she had showed me the footpath on the map.

New Year's Day. Fine and mild for walking. Winter jasmine was in flower in the garden, and along the road I saw one small but undeniable, late-blooming rose. The lawns, sloping gently towards the sea a half-mile away, were still green. Five doors down the street, in a big house set back from the row of pensioners' bungalows, lived the surgeon who had passed sentence on my mother. Who had looked down into the open cavity on the operating table and ruled the case hopeless—palliative care only recommended. His maroon Jaguar shone prosperously at me from the driveway. If I'd only brought an egg to toss on the rear window: just because.

Consider, though, a small hospital in a community of the retired, the aging, and the fact that this was a culture in which a reasonable triage came naturally. She might not have quarrelled with that decision, even. She was alone, and that depressed her; her children lived too far away. At least her doctor and the nurses were humane, and generous with Mogadon for sleeping.

The footpath, which began as a concrete gully between houses, threaded a belt of trashy woodland before reaching open country. I recognized the first farm, with stables and barn built of grey stone, handsome chestnut horses in rough winter coats out in the pasture, and here was the plank bridge over a weedy brook. The path divided, and where she and I had turned downhill the March before, this time I went up a long slope to a stile where the ploughed fields began. The ground was wet, slow going even in hiking-boots, and after an hour of picking a narrow way between thorn hedges on one side and heavy clay the color of milk chocolate on the other, I climbed a gate and sat there panting, looking for a way back to the road.

Almost at once the blue top of a car appeared, two fields over, running between the hedgerows. One forgot the small scale of this countryside, how closely it was netted with one-lane roads. There, over the rise, was the next farmhouse with its sheds and litter of machinery. The footpath must go on past it, but there was no sign, and the fields were ploughed right to the edge: so much for maintenance of the old right of way, in this season at least.

But turn to the left, where the view opened up towards the sea, and all was forgiven by grace of this undulating pattern of fields under the mild air and the fanning-out of elm or ash branches at every corner; and beyond, the light green of Pevensey Levels where pregnant sheep grazed, pearly fleeced in the sunshine. On to the road, then, and another hour's walk to Hooe village with its main pub, the Red Lion.

At the parking lot, with only fifteen minutes to closing time, I stopped short. It was crammed and overflowing with a magnificent array of antique cars, bonnets shaped like barrels strapped with leather, or like boxes hinged lengthwise with elaborate brass fittings, elaborately constructed radiator grilles, hood ornaments to die for, running boards, jump seats—everything polished and enameled to perfection. Hard to calculate the fortune in money that this assembly of vintage tech represented—though it must be in the millions, surely?—or the personal fortunes that subvented this little hobby on the side. Walking through, I heard the amplifying bay of the party inside the pub, and now remembered, New Year's Day was when the vintage cars raced from London to Brighton, and this must be an after-celebration. It wasn't even necessary for me to go inside to know what was there: the heavy-jawed faces with ruddy complexions, the heads of thick, tow-colored hair and thick necks wrapped in silk scarves, the sheepskin coats, handsewn boots, and the unmistakably declarative tone of people who'd always had things their way and claimed, without reflection, their right to dominance. The class enemy.

My mother's body language in public places retained, until her final year, the involuntary marks of social anxiety: a hyper-attentive, even fearful expression; a submissive tilt of the head and shoulders. Some other time I might have made a point of shoving inside, elbowing some space at the bar, and demanding my pint of lager and smoked-salmon sandwich. Not today. Hungry or not, I'd walk the inland road back; in any case, my mother's pantry was still full to overflowing with tins of soup, corned beef, chunk chicken, and sardines. A Christmas pudding, too, for the unheld feast.

The village, as I went through, seemed all shut in on itself, curtains drawn in the windows along the low, drab terraces. Only at the turnoff to Bexhill was there somebody on the street: a teenaged boy with cropped hair standing by his garden gate, who said in a sharp, clear voice, "*Abah! Abah!*" when I came level with him.

"Hello," I said.

"*Abah! Abah!*" He patted with one hand rhythmically along the gate and back, repeating his sound, enjoying perhaps the expulsion of breath on the second syllable. Someone called out from inside the house, and I left him to his patting of the wooden slats in sequence.

Past the houses, the road ran straight between leafless hedgerows on either side, with level fields beyond. Although it was only two-fifteen, the sun had fallen low enough to shine directly through the branchy tangle on one side, revealing the outlines of birds's nests from the season before, deep inside. So many, a whole tenement of nests! More and more kept appearing as I walked past, of different sizes and conformations, inviting me to look closer and admire the art and strategy in them. One was so closely woven, such a perfect circular basket, that I had to reach in for it. But the thing was made of fragile straws that had rotted through in the wet autumn, and it broke apart instantly. What I took, finally, thinking of the children back in Massachusetts, was a wiry little circlet made of root fibre or climbing vine, lined with a hollow of sheep's wool, that I could cut loose from its moorings with my pocket knife and carry back.

My sister arrived by car from Scotland that evening, with supplies for the reception to be held at the house next day. The service at eleven, followed by a family lunch, then the friends and neighbors at four. And by the way, she'd talked to the clergyman on the phone. He was asking if the family could give him a few words about the deceased, whom he'd met only briefly at the time her husband passed away. That chore, she implied, since I'd only bought sherry and cider and hadn't cooked, was mine to do.

We made a supper from the tinned stores and a loaf picked up from the Sunday shop, and I went into the spare bedroom to sweat out the few words for the parson. Which love should have dictated, and did so for five lines, until guilt began canceling them out.

I went into the living room. "I don't think I can do this the way it ought to be. Thing is, I've missed so much—almost twenty years."

But she was absorbed in the heavy task of making lists: what had to be done with the household goods—what shared, what donated to charity (the house itself being willed to her stepdaughter).

"Well, who else can do it? Just give it another try, love."

Back into the cold bedroom. I took the pencil and pad Mum had left in the bureau and set down in order what I could. Her early promise, those talents that circumstances of the time never allowed their proper scope or recognition. The immense labor she put into household, family—keeping her children warm and fed in wartime, nursing us through all the plagues there were before penicillin arrived. The double ordeal she endured, of losing one husband to a cruel illness, then a second. The beautiful gardens she made, and her lovely gift for friendship that blossomed early, and again late.

The clergyman read it aloud verbatim next day, at the small, discreet service, and played a tape of "Jesu, Joy of Man's Desiring" as curtains were drawn over the coffin. It was finished, but I still knew there was something absolutely vital I'd left out.

Whatever it was, it didn't come up at the cheerful restaurant lunch with our brother and his family, Auntie Mollie, and Mum's stepdaughter, remembering the best of times from the past forty-odd years and celebrating the promise of this new generation of children. Nor later, in the busywork of the reception (cakes, sandwiches, tea, sherry) for friends who had taken Mum in their cars for drives along the coast, to pub lunches in the flint-walled villages, and to the supermarket once a week.

Everyone had left by six o'clock except my sister, who would stay over to organize the disposal of the house contents; our brother would come back next day and collect papers for the solicitor. We did the washing up, and poured another glass of sherry to have with oxtail soup and a cold sandwich, sitting down to eat in the squeaky, bone-colored, vinyl armchairs which Mum had never liked after she got them six years ago—because they squeaked.

When she was done with the sandwich, my sister looked over her list and divided it in two: "O.K. There's things we'll have to deal with tonight and tomorrow. Stuff for charity, cleanout for the bins. And things the three of us'll each want to take with us or claim before the rest goes for auction."

She set her glass down and took pen in hand. Her action struck me as momentous, so that my own hand jumped slightly with the glass still in it. While I'd been alone in the house, it was as if a balance continued to be held; now I felt a wave tipping, and the vases, the mantelpiece clock, the ornaments, were all vibrating, poised to slide.

"Can we wait and do her clothes tomorrow?" I asked.

"God, yes! The thought of those maternity things she had to wear—"

She had to stop, feel for a Kleenex, before going on. "All that'll go to Oxfam; I've brought the big plastic bags. And any fresh food has to be cleared out tomorrow, too, taken or chucked. The mice, y'know?"

"What'll we get done tonight?"

"The desk mainly, papers we've to sort. Look out for any current bills."

The pigeonholes in the desk were crammed with papers, which she took out in batches and laid on the dining table.

"I'll start on these. You deal with the books; I don't know who else'd want them. And see what's in the cabinet under."

Two narrow bookshelves on each side of the desk contained exactly the same books as it had forty years ago. *Pears' Cyclopedia*, dating from the thirties: no. Kettle's *French Dictionary*, which Dad bought me secondhand for school, I would've taken, but like the bird's nest of grass, it crumbled in my hands, a wreck from hard usage. *Masterpieces of the Short Story*, 2 vols., where I was first scared by M. R. James' ghost stories and "A Terribly Strange Bed"—tempting still.

"Here's her Bible: confirmation class prize. Someone ought to have it."

"Save it for the lad," my sister said, using the old name for our brother, though he was now father of his own family. "They go to church every Sunday."

"And here's Keats, I'd forgotten."

"If you want 'em, take 'em. Otherwise they'll go to jumble."

In the cabinet were skeins of yarn, scraps of wrapping paper, and old piles of Christmas cards. (I'd received hers on that very day she'd called: fulfilling her obligations to the last.) An unused packet of notecards with wildflowers on them I offered to my sister.

"Oh," she said. "Reminds me, when I checked the drawers in her bedroom, I found all these old presents she'd never used: scent, talc, lotion. I'll never give that kind of thing again. Useless."

"Well, with scent . . . "

Here were photograph albums and old school magazines. I brought the pile over to her. "Someone really should keep these photos, don't you think? You'd be the best person, if you'd be willing."

"Why me rather than the lad, though? I mean, the man of the family."

She looked harassed, batching papers in rubber bands, shoving torn envelopes into the bin beside her.

"Well, we can see if they're up for it."

She pulled a pack of cigarettes towards her and lit one. "I'll be honest and admit I don't really care much. But I'm willing, if there's no one else."

"And these old school mags?"

"We can have a laugh before we toss 'em. One thing, though—" She pointed to the end wall of the living room. "I would like to take the Constable print and the sunflowers. I had them framed for her."

"Of course!"

Back in the hallway gloom, I dug into the right side of the cabinet and pulled out four or five plastic bags crammed with stacks of bluish-grey folded paper. Already half knowing what they were, I opened one of the ties. Oh God, no! Yes. My airmail letters to her. Nineteen years of them, sent twice or three times a month, amounting to hundreds.

My sister had once said to me, when I was back on a summer visit and told her how I enjoyed her letters, so crammed with news and comment, that she wished she could say the same about mine. "Funny, but you manage to say less in a page and a half than I'd ever have thought possible."

True, no doubt. I couldn't then explain how it all began, when I first left home and was earnestly doing my duty to the vocation—drinking as heavily as funds permitted, getting laid at every plausible opportunity, stealing books when I had no money for beer. As things got more complicated, I felt bound to lie about where I went on holidays; I manipulated addresses, names, dates; I even waylaid the postman when the legal summons in a divorce case was forwarded home, at a time when I needed to hide out there.

The pattern continued from across the Atlantic. A large percentage of what was on these hundreds of sheets of paper I *knew* to be lies—and not even inventive lies, but wretchedly bland, tedious suppressions of truth. Censored, bad-faith versions of what I'd lived through, unworthy of her and of me, both. And she'd kept every single one of them anyway, while I had at home only the last three of hers.

My sister, hearing my silence, came over to look.

"They're your letters!" she said in surprise. "Well! Of course, you might want to keep them."

"I really don't think so, y'know?"

"Well, *she* thought they were worth keeping. And they wouldn't take up much room."

I felt a frisson of resentment there dissolve into pity, and felt, too, my own panic at this evidence of my mother's tenacious faith in me as counting for something. My failure to rise to it. Even now, I might have picked them up and taken them, except for my sister, standing there.

"No, better not. I'll put them in the bin."

The dustbins by the side wall of the house were already full, but my sister was right, the bags didn't take up much room, fitting in under the lid. A fresh wind blew up the pitch-dark alley from the direction of the sea. Then water began spattering in the open drain next to my feet: my sister was making the nine-thirty cup of cocoa.

"Did I put enough cocoa in?" she asked doubtfully, handing me the mug. And to be honest, it did exhibit a faded lilac colour.

"Well, it's the way we've always had it, right?"

"Suppose so. You know, thinking about what you gave the Reverend Whatsit to read—"

"Oh—"

"Well, what you might've added, if you'd had time, was the work she did when she was married to Bill, volunteering at the Citizens' Advice. Meant a lot to her: she did it really well, I think."

That's what I missed, of course.

We finished up and went to bed by midnight. The lights were turned out, the heat turned down. Asleep or awake (and I can't be sure which was which), in those hours till dawn, I made the better account of those last fourteen years of her life. What rank egotism on my part, to have made so much of my guilt and her going under, in my imagined drama, "Seduced and Abandoned"! It's true she was bitter on my account for a long time, and she did turn on me once and say, "Oh, I wish now I'd taken you out of school at fifteen and put you to work. I wish I'd done that!"

Which to me was as much as saying that she wished my destruction, and I couldn't wait to be on the far side of the world from her.

But while I left, carrying my drama of resentment with me, she moved on past it. She got a job, got married again, went on holiday to Italy and to Greece, and in retirement did the best work of her life. Not only that: she lived her last year impeccably, with minimal complaint, firmly refusing to discuss what could not be helped—her dying. Although I loved her, it had been hard to admire the unsatisfied, fearful, thin-skinned woman (those traits I knew so well, since she passed them on to me). Now she had proved her courage, risen equal to her ending. It was with gratitude that I deferred, once and for all, to her authority.

In the morning we would be up early, stripping the beds fast while the kettle boiled. Everything here that had no definite prospect of use would go into plastic bags and join the bins outside. Our family doesn't keep things merely for the sake of keeping. We make no memorials for the dead; we let the past go. There's a troubling assumption, perhaps, that we don't deserve a place in any kind of record. That we have no history worth passing on, even to the children. Is it that there's such a predominance of women among us, still unable to feel this kind of thing matters? Only yesterday our aunt produced a handwritten sheet of paper, which the New Zealand cousins had sent over with their Christmas card to her, showing the family tree as far as they knew it, including now a Maori branch. *She* didn't want it—whatever for? Did anyone else? But no one did, until finally the emigrant's hand came forward.

The editors are right: to them it is still the same story: mixed feelings of N., sadness of M. And it's true, Dr. Johnson wrote *Rasselas* in three days to pay for his mother's funeral. This one is not for a memorial, though, since there won't be a memorial. It's only to revise and set the record a little straighter.

(Narrator strikes fist over the heart.)

Mammalia

~~~

LAST SUMMER, Anne went to do fieldwork in Indiana, some project on bats, and left her ferret with us to be taken care of. We have plenty of bats around here in Amherst, living in barns and these white carpenter's steeples. But Indiana, she said, was where they paid the right kind of attention to bats.

Anne hadn't managed to box-train the ferret: it's not a skill taught in graduate departments of biology, we gather. (But I must confess, as Anne's mother, that I hadn't managed to toilet-train *her* by the age of three; it was her visiting grandmother who showed her the sense of it.) She and I put down newspaper in all the corners of the rooms where the animal was allowed to go. Maury objected: it reminded him of the deranged household in the movie, where the woman lets piles of newspapers fill up everywhere.

"We'll get a cage," he said. "Or better, a rabbit hutch. Someone in the neighborhood must have a spare one."

Anne said absolutely no way could we put Devi in a cage. This was a creature committed to living with people. She then briefed us on the topic of ferrets, their care and feeding.

"They're not rodents; actually, they prey on rodents. They belong to the family of Mustelidae: weasels, and so on."

Well, I thought, now I know. And we were to feed it twice a day with dry kitten food, on account of its youth, keep a bowl of water nearby, and not let Genghis get at it. "That asshole cat" she called him. When Anne first arrived, she was wearing a shoulder pouch stuffed with grass slung across her stomach, and she brought out of it this loopy little creature to show Genghis—who backed up a step and then gathered himself for the killer leap. I only just caught him by the rear end. It seemed the cat, for one, included Mustelidae with rodents among his natural prey.

"There are risks to leaving it here," I told Anne. "If you can't think of a friend to take it, Cathy for instance, we might better put it in a kennel. Julia can't help out— she's going up to camp."

"I have no friends in Amherst, Mom. Zero."

"Well, then—"

"All you need to do is keep that furry sociopath away from her, O.K.? See, you can't take Devi to a kennel here: it's illegal to keep ferrets in Massachusetts."

So, I could see Maury shaking his head, *she's having us break the law, too.* Astonishing what he lets her get away with, a man at his level of security clearance. Nice trick, Anne.

For the two days that Anne stayed over with us, Genghis showed how offended he was by our treating Devi as a pet. This rank-smelling alien. He kept long and bitter watches outside Anne's door; and I remembered how the woman who sold him to us as a kitten said that a Siamese needed to be an only child, and how Julia, whose birthday present he was four years ago, answered, "That's all right. I like to think of myself as an only child, too. We'll have that in common."

Julia looked after the kitten passionately for some months, until she took up with Jordan, an elegant primate of sixteen like herself. Then Genghis revised himself into the third and always youngest of my children, each of whom seems at heart convinced of being the one and only.

The last point Anne made before taking off was that Devi had to be kept company or she'd go into a decline—bury herself in the closet and not eat. We'd have to get her up a couple of times a day and make her do things.

"What things?"

"You know, run her about the room, take her downstairs, roll her around. Give her a bath every couple of weeks, too. The way to dry her off is, you hold her up by the scruff of the neck, she goes limp, and you run the hair dryer over her for a couple minutes."

I watched Devi in Anne's bedroom, ferreting about. When it first saw you, it would freeze like a wild creature, holding its long neck up high, the button eyes staring from a small triangular head with a dark mask, the front legs in black fuzzy trousers put straight together. Its tan-colored body was low to the ground, and elongated, tipped with a black tail. Its preferences were soon clear to us: closets of junk to burrow in, upholstered furniture with holes in the back (we had plenty), and anything made of rubber, like innersoles and thongs, which it would take under the couch to chew and leave stashed until I hooked them out with a broom. Twice a day Anne gave it an hour's run in the living room, to make burrow-tracks under the rugs there, while Genghis was shut out in the kitchen.

But after she left, the animal went into a panic. It shuddered desperately in our hands when we tried to hold it and, when we put it down, jumped backwards, hissing its outrage. It got into the kitchen and slipped under the cabinets where we couldn't reach it, hiding there while Genghis tore at the screen door and howled to be let in. The ferret stayed lost in there for a whole day while I drove Julia up to the camp where she was a counselor.

She advised me: "Look, don't let Anne *exploit* you this way. If the thing ever comes out again, stick it in a cage. I've seen ferret cages in pet stores. It's easy, right?"

Late that evening, I caught sight of Devi creeping round the icebox with dust balls in its whiskers, and lunged and caught it. And stashed it in Anne's room for the duration, with extra newspapers.

We had perfect late-June weather that weekend. Maury and I hiked Mt. Monadnock one day and went canoeing on the Connecticut the next, sliding along the banks under the maples and dark hemlocks. We pulled the boat into a sandy cove, got a soda from the cooler, and climbed up to sit on the wiry grass above. Mid-morning already, when the birds go quiet and the sun on the water's too bright to look at.

"Life's good," Maury said, lying back. "We should take a proper vacation next year. Canadian Rockies, what about it?"

I thought it was a great idea.

"And," he said, "now Julia's starting college, you won't have to be a mother any more."

I wouldn't?

Monday and Tuesday I went to give the ferret some company, morning and evening, along with its kitten pellets and water, but it was always hiding deep in Anne's closet, eyes shut tight. When I pulled it out, it squirmed right back in, ignoring the food.

I spoke to Maury. "We have a problem. It's gotten depressed already."

His view was, that was just too bad. Anne had to understand we were both working: how else could we have helped fund her summer? My view was that I didn't want Devi to die on us.

"Eh! It's not gonna die." So he decided; then he flew to Nevada for a week to oversee a project at some off-limits research base. Something for the lab, related to in-space guidance systems, for which there will one day be (Maury is confident, and I don't press him on it) many civilian applications.

I work in a bookstore specializing in travel literature, local history, and a certain amount of New Age. The Pioneer Valley has always had spiritual movements. Up in the hills now there are even Buddhists; in fact, our Unitarian church hosted a session last year by a visiting lama wearing a maroon toga. His English was extremely slow and hesitant, and he went on for hours, but I remember his saying how Tibetans meditate on their mother's love for them to develop their own compassion. And that he had found many people in the West who said they couldn't bring themselves to make that meditation and who could promise to love all sentient beings *except* their mothers. He did not understand this, he admitted, but he advised us to meditate on any being from whom we had received great affection: a person, or even it might be a dog, or cat.

I was reminded of Anne, winding the ferret tenderly around her neck under her long hair.

On Thursday I came home from work to a silent house, with Maury away and no more phone calls from Julia's friends asking where she was and who she was with. I ate dinner by myself with a volume of Thoreau's *Journals* propped open on the table. The entry was from August of the year before he died, when he went camping on Monadnock and went berry picking and bathing in rocky pools, just out of sight of the day trippers. In the 1860s, the mountain must have been a gay sight, dotted over with hikers in crinolines or in cutaway coats and hats with curled brims.

Thoreau concluded his journal entries for the week's trip with a list of things he'd taken with him and how he'd revise it the next time (only there was to be no next time). He would leave out the eighteen hard-boiled eggs and take more corned beef; he'd take more sweet cake, but a less crumbly kind; take more salt, and less sugar and tea. He noted that his blanket would have been a more convenient cover if it had been stitched up in the form of a bag. Right there, he was inventing the sleeping-bag years before L. L. Bean, E. M. S., and R. E. I.

I thought of writing to Anne and offering her some of these *Journals* to read. Then, again, perhaps I shouldn't write too soon.

I have the feeling you never really liked babies that much.

It was something she had said during her latest visit. Was that actually how she put it? *I get the idea you were never much into babies . . . Well I have the idea you never really liked . . .* No, I can't recall the exact words. But I did say, when my head cleared, *Well, I don't think that's altogether right; that's not how I remember it.* And she said, *Well I mean, that's my impression, looking back.*

I wasn't going to make a big deal of it, when she was leaving again so soon. It's an awkward time, so I make allowances. But it does sting. It's as if she remembers those first months after she was born (which she couldn't, consciously), the hardest, when she never seemed to sleep more than a couple of hours at a stretch, and I got so worn out trying to understand what this intense little creature wanted that by evening I'd be almost crying with exhaustion myself. So Maury would come home, and after I'd nursed her, changed her, put her down at seven-thirty, and the crying had started over, he'd say, "Just let her cry. She has to go to sleep sometime, for Chrissake!"

And we would do that, two times out of three. She'll always forgive him—with reason, I suppose, because reason is the way he works—but why not me? The only bad mistake I know I made was not waiting longer before we had Julia. In retrospect, I'm sure we should've waited. Then there are all the other mistakes I've forgotten, repressed, or never realized for what they were . . .

I turned on the TV, then, so as not to set myself up for insomnia. Still, I was awake by six the next morning, and with time to spare before going in to work, I took my cup of coffee into Anne's room. The food and water-bowl still looked untouched. Time to talk seriously to this animal.

"Devi, you have company. I'm letting you know I'm here to wake you up."

Complete silence. (Good thing Maury couldn't hear me.) I shook the box of kitten chow. No response. I got down at the open closet door and felt in the heap of clothes Anne had said should be discarded. Some perfectly wearable shirts here that I remembered buying, smelling rather pungently now of ferret. My hand penetrated to the edge of a patch of warmth. And I had a burst of, what? Some kind of feeling that made me take an extra breath. Devi had balled herself up tightly in the fold of a Shetland sweater. I lifted her, still coiled, into a flap of my blue overshirt as I went back to Anne's armchair. After a moment, she pushed her triangular head out and yawned with a tremendous angle of gape. And then, casually, she let her chin subside onto my bare wrist.

"Oh, so it's *you* doing this to me," I murmured.

After so long, I hadn't recognized these traces of the old flame. Now Devi began stretching and twisting about, spreading the minute pads of her feet and threadlike claws in the air. My right hand was there so she wouldn't roll off, and she turned over and licked the palm of it. When she came to the fold of skin between thumb and finger, she took it in her jaws and started chewing—gently, then harder, making a faint chuckling sound in her throat.

"Enough, now; maybe you'll eat?"

And first from my damp palm, then from the dish, she ate. Maury called the next evening to ask how things were.

"Fine. I've had some quality time with the ferret; I think we'll be O.K."

That night I began sleeping in Anne's bed. I brought in my books, spare glasses, clock radio. Her room overlooks the valley, all trees and distant spires, whereas our corner bedroom, though larger, looks only towards the next-door house and the Pelham road. After the light was out, I heard squeaking for a while as Devi savaged a partially-inflated balloon (I'd bought a supply of these from the dimestore, on Anne's advice). It ceased; then I felt a light scrabbling move onto the bed and the brush of her drooping whiskers along my arm before she burrowed under the covers. I'd been warned about her habit of chewing on bare toes and the backs of knees, and pulled my feet up preemptively; but she was quickly on her way out the other end.

In the grey dawn I woke to hear her crunching on the food and Genghis complaining on the other side of the bedroom door. Poor cat. I might have to shut him in the kitchen for the time being. And I drowsed again, thinking vaguely about the way a person might not be the best mother for a given child. For instance, if my cousin Miriam and I could have switched our firstborns (they were only five months apart), we might have done better. Anne could have used someone more organized—she thrived on the pressure—but Miriam drove Steven crazy for just those reasons, and the latest news was that he'd dropped out of college a third time and gone to live in a shack belonging to some ski-bum friends near Boise, Idaho. Forever, he said.

The radio came on: I must have slept, because it was seven already, and Devi was rolled up in the hollow next to me.

All afternoon at the bookstore I watched the clock, anxious to be going home, remembering Devi's scratching at the door when I left her locked in. Then Maury called that night, and I broke the news to him about having to sleep in Anne's room. "It seems like the only solution, if I'm to keep her healthy and eating."

"Well, it seems pretty extreme to me," he said.

I mentioned an alternative possibility: bringing Devi and her gear into our room.

"Not a *chance!*" he said. "I'm not having newspapers; I don't want the smell. And if it bites toes when you're asleep, what else is it going to bite? I'm sorry, but you'll have to make a choice here."

I'd already chosen. When he got home, I had a compromise

worked out: I'd sleep Tuesday to Friday in Anne's room, taking care of Devi, and weekends with Maury. There was no discussion, other than his saying it was ridiculous and my agreeing completely and shrugging because there was nothing else to be done. He put up with the arrangement in silence, except once when I came out of the bathroom in the morning with Devi over my shoulder and met him in the hallway.

"Can't you take a shower without that animal for company?"

"God, Maury, it's not that. It's that Genghis got into Anne's room. He's under the bed, wouldn't come out, so I had to take this one with me."

"You know what that cat does at night now?"

"No, what?"

"He's taken your place. Sleeps right there with his head on your pillow."

Brilliant Genghis! "That's kind of sweet of him, no?"

Maury did crack a brief smile. But it was only a matter of time before the ferret got into his running shoes and stole a rubber insert, and we were in worse trouble. Julia, too, after calling up and talking to him first, jumped on my case.

"It's the same story all over again, Mom. You have to kick this doormat habit, you know?"

I let her finish, then told her not to worry herself, because Devi was going back on August twenty-third. When I looked at the calendar, I saw that was only six days off. So quick, I thought, and went straight up to Anne's room to sit on the floor next to where Devi was shaped into her perfect circle on the armchair, tail scarfed under her chin. And those neat, round ears—no human baby could compete in that department.

As it happened, when her field project ended, Anne hitched a ride from Indiana to Connecticut via New York. She called when she arrived and said we could either keep Devi a week longer, till she could borrow a car to come up, or one of us could drive her down. But it was clear which I'd better do.

My last evening with Devi, I walked her in the yard to see the moon and a few late fireflies, then let her run around on the screen porch. A few moths had got inside the screens; I caught one for her, which she pounced at and ate alive, crunching it like popcorn. Maury stood and watched this from the doorway to the living room.

"Let it go," I said. "O.K.?"

In the morning the ferret was wide awake, sniffing the changed atmosphere as I lined the carrier with newspaper and Anne's old sweater. She flicked away when I reached for her, and ran under the bed. By now I had learned to sprinkle a few more pellets in the food bowl and sit there until her circular wanderings brought her, sadly, within range. In the carrier she put her front feet up on the mesh and stared anxiously. I poked a deflated balloon through to distract her, and some cat treats from Genghis's stash, picked up the bag with her gear, and we left. The day was humid, promising discomfort; I felt, too, oddly premenstrual, although three months ago the gynecologist had been confident I was done with all that. So much for the promised easy trip through.

I drove fast: this New England peneplain country always bored me, with its tree-fuzzed hills all the same height so there was no commanding view anywhere. At Hartford we were ten minutes ahead of schedule, and it wasn't yet noon when I pulled up at the shabby, three-decker house with its many doorbells. A young woman I didn't know opened the door. Like many of the students here, she was good-looking in the way these elite places seem to recruit them, with a mane of hair and a version of that Hemingway jawline.

Was Anne there? I asked.

"Oh, you're her mom. Sorry, she had to be at the lab. She said you'd be dropping off Devi."

She put her hand out for the carrier, but I thought *No, not like that.*

"I'll just carry it in, O.K.? Maybe you could show me the room."

For a moment I really thought she was going to refuse. Then she said sure, fine with her. Upstairs was a warren of student rooms, strewn with broken-gutted armchairs, odd plants. A ferret's paradise, no doubt. Anne's own room was tidily kept: here was her flute on the bookcase, her small but choice fossil collection on the bureau. I spread out the newspapers from my bag in the corners, got water from the unspeakable kitchen sink, and at last took Devi out of the carrier and stroked her in the crook of my arm, where she trembled a little.

"This is home, Devi. You'll remember."

The young woman in the doorway swung one long leg patiently across the other. Anne had left a flannel shirt on the bed, ready for Devi to be tucked into, and I did that and went out past the roommate, pulling the door closed.

"Best to keep her in one room for a few hours."

"Sure."

"And please tell Anne 'hello' from me."

"Sure, O.K."

"I thought I might take her to lunch, but I guess not this time."

"I guess."

So I've done what Anne asked us to do, and must do no more. These are tough people to deal with, I think. And why is that, do they know? Is it that we should've had no children at all, or else more of them—enough so that we wouldn't have to carry around this burden of love for just the one, or two, like some toxic stuff that's so strong it mustn't spill over?

In any case, I must stop at the Friendly's before the highway, for an iced tea and a tuna melt, and to get myself together. For heaven's sake, where's the tragedy? Miriam, I know for a fact, would give anything to have Steven going to grad school. An arm, a leg, a breast—*anything*. So I'll drink my iced tea for a few minutes, before getting on the road and going home to make it all right with poor Genghis, and with Maury. An extra minute for me, also, to think about Anne coming back to her room this evening, with Devi there as promised.

There was a nurse on the maternity ward where she was born who carried her to me with such a look of affection and pleasure that I asked, "Do you have children of your own?"

And she said, "Just the one. But you know how it is: when I'm not with the one I love, I love the one I'm with."

That seedy old song, sure, I know it well.

My Very Own Jew

~~~

TAKING THIS VACATION, Audrey knew, was something their friends could interpret as ill-treatment of an already beleaguered husband. *London, indeed!* they were surely thinking. *Is she quitting altogether, going back home?*

But she thought, *Hell, it's only two weeks.* A modest enough return for all that Ira—and, let's add, the universe at large—had put her through in the past year.

What she really wanted was to be able to live with Ira afterwards in some kind of balance. A mean little strategy for a better end. Because that line from Sondheim's *Company* which she'd once delivered in a community theater production—"At last, my very own Jew!"—still counted for much. The life he'd brought her, meaning a liberation from those Christian constraints on mind and body, as well as the only decent kind of politics in America: the heritage of Emma Goldman, Paul Goodman, Irving Stone. All that, and twenty-five years together. (But it had to occur to her, maybe she'd never quite grasped the way it appeared from his side; maybe the deal was never evenly balanced?)

He'd let her know he didn't appreciate her going off this way. Not for nothing did his parents (may they rest in peace and forgive Audrey her imitation *Yiddishkeit*) call him Ira: anger. Well now, she figured, taking the Yellow Cab to the airport, everyone's got something to forgive.

Her first evening in London, Audrey got a brusque reminder of the unmerciful ways of her native place: sitting after dinner face-to-face with Marianne, she caught her dear friend leaning slantwise on an elbow, looking past her, and checking her own reflection in the dark window behind. Did she look worse than her old mate after all these years? Better? About the same? And Audrey wanted to tell her, *No, don't do that, listen to me!*

Marianne couldn't know that the gesture was so like what Audrey had caught her lovely young woman doctor doing, right after she'd found the lump and handed out the order for the breast clinic. At the time, Audrey was sitting against a mirrored-glass wall in the examination room, with Dr. Lin facing. And the doctor's involuntary shift to her own reassuring image in the mirror behind the patient—clear, pale skin, black-olive eyes, etc.—made damningly clear how much she wished this depressing transaction were over.

When the results came back O.K., Dr. Lin remarked with charming candor that she wasn't too surprised: the lump hadn't had that kind of *gritty* feel to it.

"Gritty. . . ?"

"Yeah, cancer tends to feel kind of, you know, pebbly? Gritty? Yours had slightly different texture, more rubbery."

"I see."

"So, everything fine for now! Relax!"

That's when Audrey went home and called the discount travel people, to get away. And now here was her best, oldest friend from the days of working together in the Golders Green bookshop, when they had lived on bacon-and-veggie stew. Here was her duty-free Jack Daniel's between them on the kitchen table, and here Marianne had her little hash pipe out and her gay lodger, Jake, just came down to share it. At that point, Audrey brought up "the Ira problem," only to see Marianne's attention slipping away, over her shoulder to the window.

At least Jake picked up. "Oh, *men!*" he wailed, in his resonant alto. "Sluts, all of them. *Tell* me about it! I mean last night, who pops out of the bushes at me, leaving the pub? Only the Booker Prize man himself—*well hello there!* Married, three kids at *least*—what can you do?"

"What *did* you do?" Marianne's focus was back.

Blessing him, Audrey leaned over to freshen his drink.

"Only what *you'd* do, my dear," he said, "if you'd got two-and-a-half unpublished novels sitting at home. He's nicer than his pictures, anyway."

Jake flipped a dangle of chestnut hair. They all laughed, and Marianne passed a hand over her one-inch crop, peppered brown and silver. Audrey, illuminated by that easy hilarity, wondered why she and Ira hadn't noticed the problem of a heterosexual life without gay friends. It was a fucking desert wilderness—what prevented them from seeing that? Ira's being in the sciences was partly to blame, but surely, surely they could've looked. She had acquaintances, at least, in the university library, yet never reached out.

Then another look at Marianne, and Audrey suddenly clicked that this was the first time in thirty years she'd seen the real color of her friend's hair. What happened?

"Oh this, well, it's one of my *pujas* I'm doing this year."

"You were platinum when you left Roddy, I remember."

"My first husband," she told Jake. "Oh God, yes. And 'course, I had to go on being blond as long as I was with David—oh, very much the loyal *shiksa*, darling, wearing my fingers down to the bone, stuffing cabbage, chopping liver—"

Jake began singing "What I Did for Love."

"Even Audrey, here, went blond for Ira, didn't you sweetie? Confess! I've got her wedding photo. Frightfully sixties—oh, acres of cotton eyelet and barefoot in the grass."

Audrey couldn't deny it. They'd been brides the same year, on opposite shores of the Atlantic. Only Marianne gave it up after switching to ceramics and the fight against racism; she took a series of lovers, ending with handsome Alex from Trinidad, who moved in for ten years of pig's feet stew and curried goat *rotis*. The only thing Marianne held onto was the house, which her Dad had given her after her first divorce. David was long gone to Canada, and their son was through college. Now Marianne was deep into meditation, which didn't preclude the occasional dose of cigarettes, hash, and whiskey.

While all that fun was happening, Audrey was going West with

Ira, by stages. She started her doctorate in Madison, because he taught there, finished it at UC–Los Angeles, and she stayed the *shiksa*.

But not blond. Blond no more.

"The two of you look *so* like sisters," Jake told her. "I'd swear you were sisters."

"We knew that," Marianne said. "Always did. I mean, it's obvious."

On her side of the table, the peppered crop and the all-black cotton layers, hung with Nepalese silver and a bone necklace. On Audrey's, the longer brown crop, navy warm-ups, sneakers for traveling, and silver hoops. The ever-rosy complexion they shared and the bad teeth. The surprise to Audrey was how, in their mutual turn towards austerity, they'd come to resemble a pair of post–Vatican II religious types, except for the shoes and the jewelry. It was just a more florid order that Marianne belonged to: whereas Audrey's bedroom was all off-white furniture, with the standard TV/VCR and video rack underneath, Marianne's featured a gorgeously draped alcove with its bronze Himalayan image, bowls of flowers, rice, and water, and purple cushion. And there was her velvet-quilted bed, with three beautiful spotted Egyptian cats, half-grown, nested warmly together in the aura of incense.

With Marianne, the celibacy of her middle age was honored by a shrine of spiritual and sensory riches. Ira had called her "one of those minority-of-the-month girls," but that was unfair. What Audrey saw was the fate of a younger sibling, much like herself: the unsponsored and restless one. Marianne's older sister took a brilliant degree and went into the Board of Trade, even as Marianne dropped out of art school to become the wife of a car dealer before she turned twenty-one. (*Well somebody has to marry the buggers,* she used to say.) Just as Audrey's own sister rose to be dean of her nursing school, while Audrey was half in college, half trying her damnedest to become an alcoholic, until she met Ira at a New Left gathering in Earl's Court.

As for their own marriage, which began in a Vermont orchard hung with more red apples than branches ought to bear, Audrey had come to see in it a kind of liminal settlement, beginning there in the outdoors. A campsite on the margins of each other's identity. Ira had wanted out of the tight community of Temple Beth Yaacov (but perhaps not all the way?), and she wanted out of St. Michael's parish, Bexleyheath (but did it have to be quite so far?). They were uncannily like the alley cats they also kept, forever couching in the doorway.

Audrey talked to Ira in her mind. *Confess it, baby, you always thought Marianne something of a fool, but this year has made bigger fools of both of us.* He, getting himself publicly suspended from the lab for what Marianne said the French called "Zizi Pompon." She, herself, by extension, the sorry-ass wife, in the wrong whatever she did: either a gender traitor if she backed him or, in the eyes of most of their friends, a bitch if she didn't.

"Did he do it, then?" Marianne finally asked her.

Audrey said, well, she assumed of course something happened— sure, some kind of inappropriate whatever. As opposed to appropriate.

Marianne laughed, came 'round the table, and kissed her on both cheeks. "Never mind, kiddo, happens to the best, don't you know? Look at Sogyal Rinpoche, who wrote that marvelous book. *He* was done for the old sexual harassment, too, wasn't he?"

So Audrey poured them a last shot and gave out her presents. For Marianne, a Navajo bracelet, and for Jake, at random, a personals column she'd clipped from the alternative student paper at the state college and found stashed in her bag on the flight over.

Jake opened up the page and brightened instantly.

"'Dear Tray,'" he started quoting, "'I like your dick, but really! Try zipping it up once in a while, or I'll haveta stop beating you off and beat you up.' How totally charming! 'Anyways'—Was that a misprint? Not? O.K.—'I got the KY jelly for you, my little cavity of love, so prepare yourself. Sincerely, your own BJ.' This is *marvelous!* But Audrey, love, *what* is that 'sincerely' doing here?"

"Well, Jake, you mightn't think it, but these are well-brought-up, middle-class kids."

He smoothed the paper out on the table and read on.

"Oh, this one's harsh! 'To the annoying Asian chick in Poli Sci: *Shut up!* We are not amused by your Third World showing-off. Go to the Prof's office hours if you want to kiss ass. You are driving me BUGSHIT! I swear, you make me want to stick frozen Mentos up your crack. So quit while there's still time!—From a concerned student in the class.' But here's that little valediction again. *Concerned*, isn't it sweet?"

Marianne started working some pressure points on her skull and said, hell, it was clear nothing whatever on the racism front had changed in all these years.

At least, wasn't there more prejudice *diversity*? Audrey asked. If Jake would give her the clipping a moment, she could demonstrate.

But he wouldn't, not right away. "'I'm a nubile seductress trapped in a hairy six-foot man's body,'" he read musingly. "This is one hot college! Any chance you could get me in?"

She leaned over and grabbed. "This is what I mean, Mari. 'Hey bitch with the nappy-ass hair in the front row of Physics discussion! Who the fuck d'ya think you are, making eyes at my man, Humberto? Shit, you'd be lucky to get laid by that fat sweaty nerd with the laptop. Damn, with those banana tits and those four HUGE zits on your forehead, Geezus! I'm surprised you don't give the TA a stroke. *Tienes las pechas de una vaca. Hijole!*'"

Jake shook his head in admiration. "What *voice!* It's got eloquence, it's *melody*!"

And Audrey to Marianne: "See, I used to claim Brits were the most offensive bigots in the world, but now we might as well give up."

"Still, seeing everything that's gone down in this country under Thatcher, it'd destroy me if I didn't have the teachings. The Dharma."

The bottle was empty now; Jake took off upstairs, and the two of them went to unroll the futon in the back room where Audrey would sleep. The place looked in bad shape, cracks zigzagging the plaster around the window, and tumbled heaps of stuff on the floor. It had been a long descent from Marianne's childhood, in the manor house with its walled garden at Hambledon. Yet she'd never lost an implicit faith in the next wave of possibility; and if you didn't have a regular job, you were all the more free to catch it.

"Where can we go this week?" she asked, standing at the door, consulting the mysterious oracle of herself. "There's so few days. Still, we *could* run down to cousin Rupert's cottage at Moggers. He isn't there except for August and Bank Holidays."

Mid-June, she said, was perfect. Nobody around. Take down a nice load of scoff from Waitrose. Bottle of claret, a piece of game pie, etc. Drive down Wednesday, back Saturday to go to the theatre. She'd phone Rupert in the morning. And Jake would look after the cats.

After breakfast they took off in Marianne's red Citroën, which she still drove in the style of the pro racer who taught her when she was seventeen, cutting classes to go screw with him out in the fields.

Moggeswell was a village hidden among trees under the southern slope of the Downs, a few miles inland from Worthing. Her cousin's cottage was old whitewashed brick, and from its upper windows you could see the high beeches of Chanctonbury Ring. Audrey remembered, from a visit twenty years back, a long downstairs room that opened through French doors into the flower garden edged with boxwood, which gave off a scent always linked for her with summer heat.

She watched Marianne running her hand along the knapped flints in the side wall, feeling for where the doorkey was hidden behind a loose flint; and in the same moment, a line started running in her head, exactly as it had the first time she'd waited on that path: "*The lost traveller's dream under the hill.*"

After the one line came back, another surfaced, while Marianne's hand still teased at the stones:

The son of morn in weary day's decline,
The lost traveller's dream under the hill.

Blake's Lucifer. The son of morn: *like you Ira*, she thought, *all gone into eclipse the past five years, the projects closing down one by one as grant money dried up. And then who betrayed whom? The damn profession let you down, didn't it? So you turned around and let it down, as well.*

They might be pressuring him, after the forced leave of absence, to take early retirement: he'd be fifty-nine in September. An absolute disaster.

All of twenty-two she was, the woman who brought the grievance. A senior. Audrey had seen only the newspaper shot, the windblown hair—yes, blond—and tight jeans. And her complaint: that she was coerced into sex with this senior professor, director of the lab, because he was supervising her graduate-student boyfriend at the time, who was known to be having difficulties. She claimed that Ira knew all along the guy was her boyfriend, which was plausible, in the close environment of the lab.

And you were iron-faced, Ira. Said you never knew anything about a boyfriend, and you thought—could it really be an honest mistake?—that she was coming on to you.

The predictable settlement left everybody smeared. Ira pleaded guilty to "poor judgment," the well-known moment of madness in the coffee lounge after hours. The girl, herself, had admitted a measure of complicity. The department found a way to give the boyfriend his Ph.D. in a hurry. And Ira got his slap on the wrist.

Audrey could see that lounge so clearly, every time the humiliation broke over her. She saw those aluminum windows you can't open, with the vertical plastic blinds, the paper cups and coffee machine on the steel credenza, the vinyl-tile floor. The same scene in all institutions—that foam couch, too, upholstered in speckled neutrals. Hateful place, bloody beige steel credenzas! She would like to die before ever seeing such another coffee lounge again. But she should be so lucky . . .

And meanwhile their boys, away at grad school, were struck virtually dumb—could scarcely imagine what to say to either parent.

Marianne got the cottage door open. Inside, it was so profoundly quiet, Audrey wanted to apologize for her mind's disturbance. Light filtered down from upstairs and through an open door at the end of the passage. A tall clock opposite the stairs ticked slowly.

"Used to be glowworms in the garden," Audrey said.

One clear night, that first time here, they'd been drinking outside on the grass and had become aware of a green luminescence by the path. But Marianne said she'd not seen glowworms in years. Everything here had changed drastically for the worse. There was a Cabinet Minister living in the next village; their pub was infested with journalists and security. You saw sick foxes on the roads. Overweight magpies had eaten up the songbirds. All gone to pot.

Declaring herself knackered after the drive, Marianne went to take a nap upstairs. Audrey stashed food in the fridge and checked out the pantry. Rupert kept minimal stores: tea, sugar, steak sauce, biscuits in a tin, and a bottle of Ribena. She poured a purple shot into a glass and diluted it. The drink of childhood, a syrupy treat.

Outside, it was clear someone had been working: the lawn was shaved, the borders of pinks and lavender weeded, tall delphiniums staked alongside the phlox. A mauve buddleia bush simmered with small butterflies. Framed by rose bushes, it divided the flowers from the vegetable garden behind: an immemorial order, like the silence kept by songbirds resting in the middle of the day.

On the drive, Marianne had offered her the old life back again. "You could live upstairs in the house, any time. Jake's got a lover he could move in with. There's loads of jobs you could get. Think about it, eh?"

Audrey, studying the way the village houses fit into the folds of the land, reached out a grateful hand.

"God, Marianne, when I see these houses, you've no idea how *temporary* places look, over there. Throw up a balloon frame of two-by-fours, add Sheetrock and siding, or spray on stucco—that's it. Multiply by a hundred, a hundred thousand. The apartment building in New York where Ira and I first lived together—a few years later I was driving by, it was just a hole in the ground. Typical."

"Well, it's all *maya*, isn't it Aud? Same impermanence."

"I know, but there it's *in your face*, all the time. Here, you can arrive at a realization: oh, this is *maya*. It doesn't run you over at eighty miles an hour, every day, soon as you get up in the morning."

Audrey walked the length of the garden, observing beyond the flower beds rows of peas, carrot fronds, lettuce. At the tall hedge in back, she turned. Dappled shade was advancing over the lawn, from what she might once have called the neighbor's copse, or spinney. (But did she ever know the right terms?) Time, soon, to go inside.

The only book she had in her carry-on bag was a volume of Chekhov, containing his story of a child's summer journey across the steppe. She would have to teach it, come September, and confront Chekhov's self-damning reference to "that peculiar oily brilliance of his eyes which is found only in Jews." On that evidence (and there was more), even Saint Chekhov couldn't help being revolted by the marks of the alien—couldn't help preferring his own peculiar nation, with their blessedly oil-free eyes.

Where *did* that "oily" come from? Was it like the Mediterranean "olive complexion," deriving somehow from the olive groves—not to mention the Mount of Olives—and why not take a wild leap from there? As for the phrase "found only in Jews," what could one say, except where was the good doctor's grasp of physiology, or the experienced traveler's eye? It was so ludicrous, so damn creepy. And in another moment Audrey was sitting on Rupert's lawn, inlaid with those daisies that grew only here, and admitting—no, *embracing*—the whole pathology herself. Yes, *yes!* In tears, even, with the craving to regress back to her own bloody kind, oh *very* bloody indeed! Her appalling, comfortable, and unforgivable kind: notorious slavers and exploiters, pious mass-murderers by knives, axes, guns, ropes, burning, drowning, and the starvation of millions, starting for convenience's sake with the Welsh and Irish and Scots and going on to the rest of the world. But who cared, finally—every nation did it—just, please, give her back her own god-damned filthy *raza*!

Marianne called from the kitchen, while Audrey was still blotting her eyes with travel Kleenex. She was assembling her version of high tea, with Harrods' game pie, a granary loaf, and would Audrey please pull a bunch of lettuce from the garden. It was, she said from the doorway, their duty to eat Rupert's lettuce, since when lettuce was *à point*, somebody should see it wasn't let go to waste. And they didn't.

Then, to the pub for best bitter and a game of table-skittles, and the half-mile walk back to the cottage while the sky was still light after sunset, with a new moon high between the elms, and the rooks in the churchyard colony were still kvetching on.

"Tomorrow," said Marianne, "I'll make Rupert's curry—he always has the stuff in the fridge. Which reminds me, Aud, one day you've got to come shopping in New Delhi—fantastic! First, we'll go up to Dharamsala, the teachings for a month, and there's huge, dramatic thunderstorms coming over the peaks, because it's the rainy season, and you're sitting in the courtyard for eight-hour sessions, totally drenched, mud *everywhere*, and magically happy. Then, on the way out, we do major shopping—*perfect!* You know, someday you'll have to do it, Aud."

Late at night, with Rupert's bottle of Glenlivet between them, Marianne told her why that was so. During a retreat the image had come to her, with total clarity, of the two of them together with a third friend in some past time, boy novices in a monastery that she could describe exactly, down to the precise crimson color of the painted beams in the temple, so that her lama could name the actual site in Tibet, and even the period—around the eleventh century. And they had taken their bodhisattva vows together there, which guaranteed their return, and remeeting, life after life, until the end of time.

Taking this in, Audrey wondered aloud, what about Ira, and Marianne's David? And the children? Were they ever in the picture? Or were Jews conceivably exempt from reincarnation, because of the weight of their sufferings? Or as yet another mark of singularity? Marianne thought not, but often enough a spouse in the present life turned out to have been one's parent or child in another.

Well, that figured, once you thought about it.

At nearly midnight, Audrey went upstairs to the second bedroom, with its narrow bookshelf containing handbooks on canine breeds, back issues of investment magazines, and a book left over maybe from Rupert's childhood: *Wonder Tales.* Though tired, she pulled this one out; it fell open to a Rackham-style illustration of a forest path on which two figures were riding.

The story is also told, she read, *of a great king who possessed many treasures, none more precious to his heart than his beautiful wife. Until one day when, out hunting in his forests, he stopped to rest in the heat of noon beside a waterfall. Having drunk from the cool stream, and eaten, he lay down to sleep, watched over by his followers. Some time later, as in a dream, he overheard a voice speak, under the rushing of the waters:*

"While our king here rests, his wife labors mightily, pleasuring the foul cook in his kitchens. But who dares undeceive him?"

The king lay still as if stung by an adder, but gathering his senses together, he stretched his limbs and arose as if he had heard nothing. Leaving his followers, he took with him one loyal squire and rode straight to his castle, where he found—alas!—that the voice had spoken truly. There and then he cut the throats of the adulterous pair with his hunting knife.

But having done so, he found no satisfaction or relief from the misery that had beset him ever since he heard the fatal voice. He determined to hand over the governance of the kingdom to his vizier, and set out with his squire to wander the roads, in quest of finding one woman of perfectly attested virtue and honor . . .

Where the page ended it was enough, time to sleep. The birds of the village would start up again by three-thirty, midsummer nights at this latitude being so short. Even as she put down the book and turned off the frilly bedside lamp, a cock crowed somewhere. Marianne heaved a sighing breath from the other room. Next day the two of them, friends for almost ten centuries, would go over to Worthing for a walk by the seaside and a fish supper.

Audrey talked a little more to Ira in her head, saying she hadn't come here looking for a better man, or woman, either, although she could hear his voice laying down the bad news: "*Sorry, Aud, it's just men or women, that's the sum total of possibilities.*" And she improvised the continuing train of his answer, that every man is marked from the beginning in these unalterable ways, and every woman is marked in other ways, and people never really change, do they?

She will come back to you, Ira, and bear with your incurable and never quite understood scars and complaints; as you may bear with her own, just as intractable and resistant to the mind. You both chose a stranger to live with and must have wanted some strangeness to persist.

Audrey is imagining for the last third of her life a braided delta of selves, all of whom are flowing together and apart and together, through space and time. This picture, Marianne's wild gift, will be her peaces, though she may keep it closeted for the sake of yours.

There's a gust of wind against the cottage, and a sporadic patter of rain following it. Tomorrow Audrey and Marianne, the Tibetan boys, will get up and see the mist rising through the hilltop beeches and, later, walk on the beach.

ACKNOWLEDGMENTS

Earlier versions of some of these stories appeared in the following journals: *Faultline, New England Review, North American Review, Ploughshares, Santa Monica Review, TriQuarterly, Village Voice,* and *Yale Review.*

My first thanks go to Allen Grossman: partner, conscience, and unnamed presiding spirit in "Great Teacher." Thanks also to generous readers Pat Goodheart, Jean McGarry, Lynne Tillman; to my former colleagues and students at the University of California–Irvine, Warren Wilson College, and the University of Iowa, for the best kind of challenge. I'm especially grateful to John Irwin for the advice of an impeccable editor. And to Adam Grossman, for the musical cue. Lastly, to Bathsheba, Austin, and Lev Grossman, and my family and friend Bridget in the U.K. I offer thanks for all the worlds they have opened up for me, and an *apologia* for this book, as a small return on great gifts.